ALLEN&UNWIN

First published in 2002

Allen & Unwin
83 Alexander Street
Crows Nest NSW 2065
Australia
Phone: (61 2) 8425 0100
Fax: (61 2) 9906 2218
Email: info@allenandunwin.com
Web: www.allenandunwin.com

National Library of Australia
Cataloguing-in-Publication entry:

Wright, Joshua, 1973– .
  Plotless, pointless, pathetic.

  For children.
  ISBN 1 86508 785 8.

  I. Title.

A823.4

Cover and text design by Tou-Can Design
Set in 13.5 pt Tiepolo Book by Tou-Can Design
Printed by McPherson's Printing Group, Maryborough, Victoria

10 9 8 7 6 5 4 3

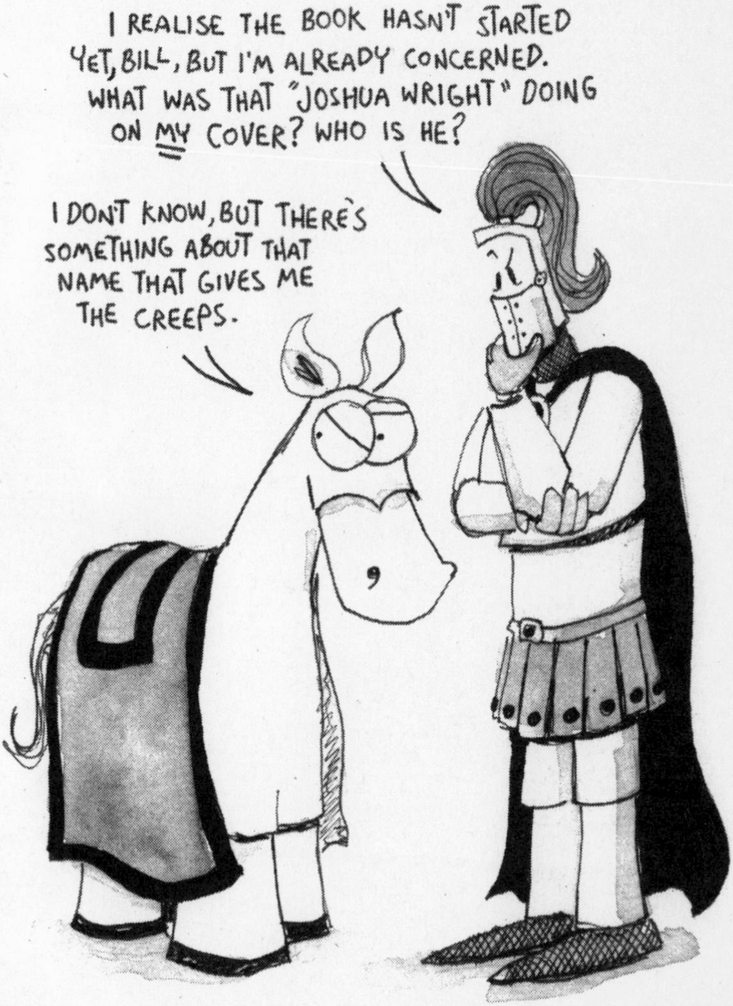
I REALISE THE BOOK HASN'T STARTED YET, BILL, BUT I'M ALREADY CONCERNED. WHAT WAS THAT "JOSHUA WRIGHT" DOING ON MY COVER? WHO IS HE?
I DON'T KNOW, BUT THERE'S SOMETHING ABOUT THAT NAME THAT GIVES ME THE CREEPS.

Chapter One

Do you know who this is? If you don't, you should. He is the hero of this fantastic book you're about to read. His name is Sir Glame and he's a knight.

I AM BRIMMING OVER WITH GOODNESS AND NOBILITY.

Sir Glame's hobbies include killing bad things with his sword,

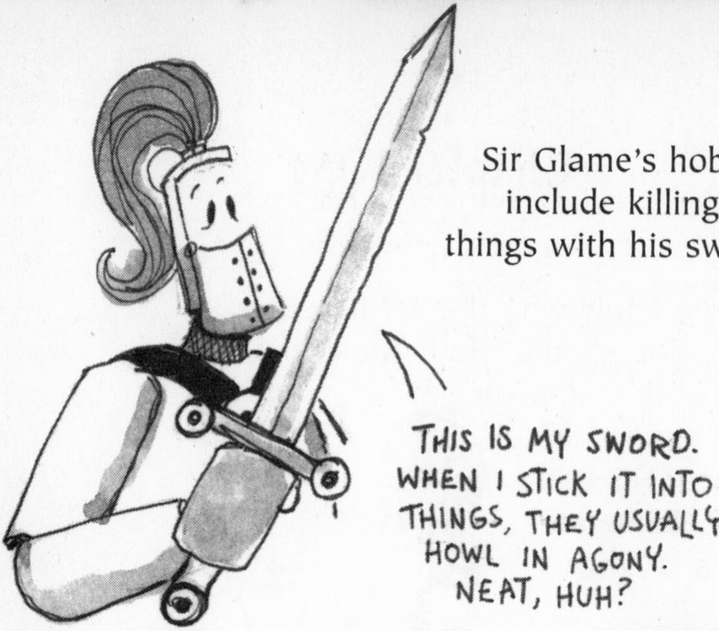
THIS IS MY SWORD. WHEN I STICK IT INTO THINGS, THEY USUALLY HOWL IN AGONY. NEAT, HUH?

rescuing damsels,

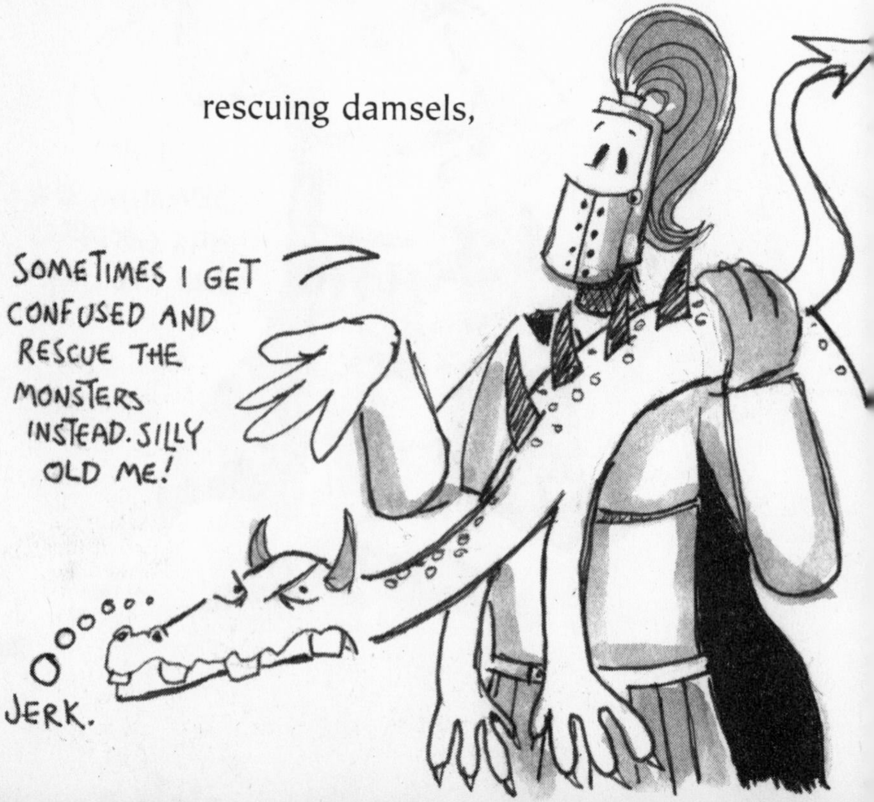
SOMETIMES I GET CONFUSED AND RESCUE THE MONSTERS INSTEAD. SILLY OLD ME!
JERK.

swinging on ropes hanging over dangerous chasms (preferably filled with lava), and generally feeling pretty pleased with himself. He also enjoys candlelit dinners, walking in the rain, and aerobics.

A PIT FULL OF PUPPIES? I CAN'T SWING ACROSS THIS. IT'S JUST NOT DANGEROUS ENOUGH.

This here is Bill.

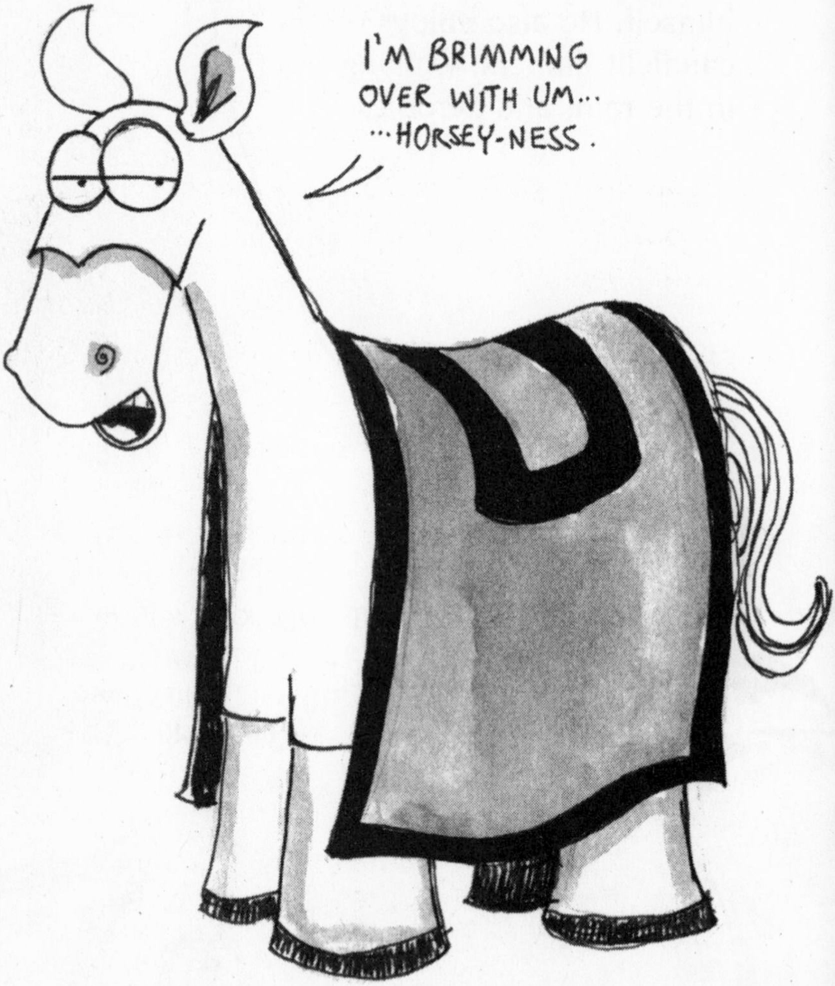
I'M BRIMMING
OVER WITH UM...
...HORSEY-NESS.

When Sir Glame chooses not to use his legs, he rides a horse. Bill is his trusty steed. Bill's hobbies include sleeping a lot, trying to look busy, making fun of things, and being too clever for his own good. He also enjoys candlelit dinners, but doesn't like rain and thinks aerobics is the invention of an overweight madman.

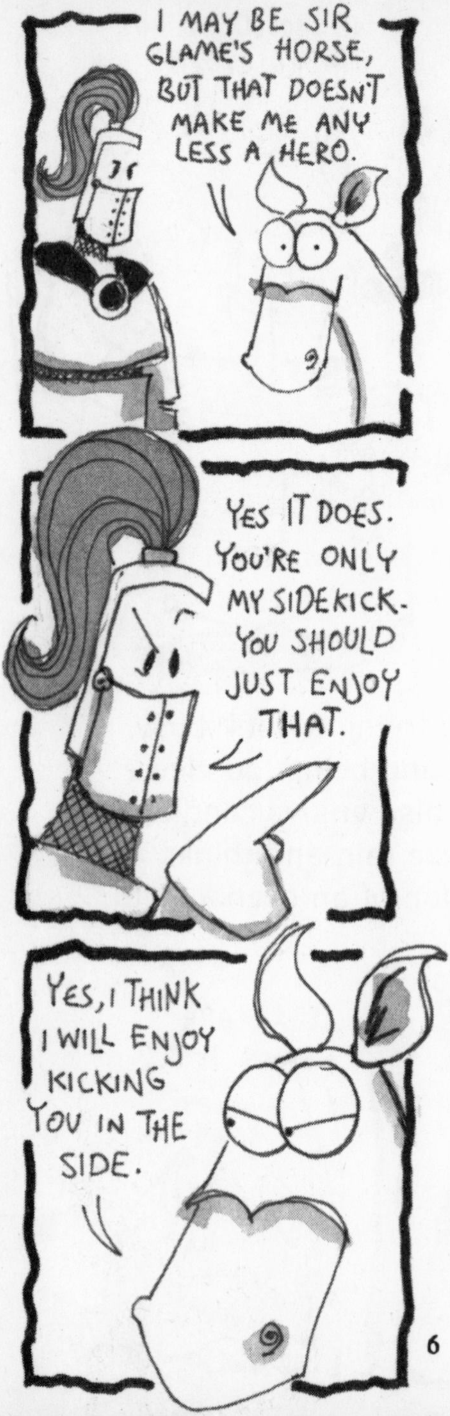
I MAY BE SIR GLAME'S HORSE, BUT THAT DOESN'T MAKE ME ANY LESS A HERO.
YES IT DOES. YOU'RE ONLY MY SIDEKICK. YOU SHOULD JUST ENJOY THAT.
YES, I THINK I WILL ENJOY KICKING YOU IN THE SIDE.

So, just to recap what we've learned:

1. Sir Glame will be the knight hero of this story.
2. Bill will be the horse.

There – that's all you really need to know. The rest of this book may make no sense at all, but as long as you cling to those two rules, you'll be okay.

Sir Glame and Bill lived in a far-off fantasy kingdom. The kind that had dragons, princesses, towering castles, creepy woods full of wolves and houses made out of confectionary.

YOU KNOW, I'M NOT EVEN WEARING ANY UNDERWEAR. I FEEL SO FREE!

DISGUSTING!

PRUDISH PIXIE.

There were wizards and witches and plenty of talking animals who always wore jackets but never any pants. Yes, it was the kind of fairytale land you've read about a million times before.

I SALUTE THE GOOD OLD RED, WHITE AND SAUSAGE.

Sir Glame and Bill's particular kingdom went by the name of Sausagopolis.

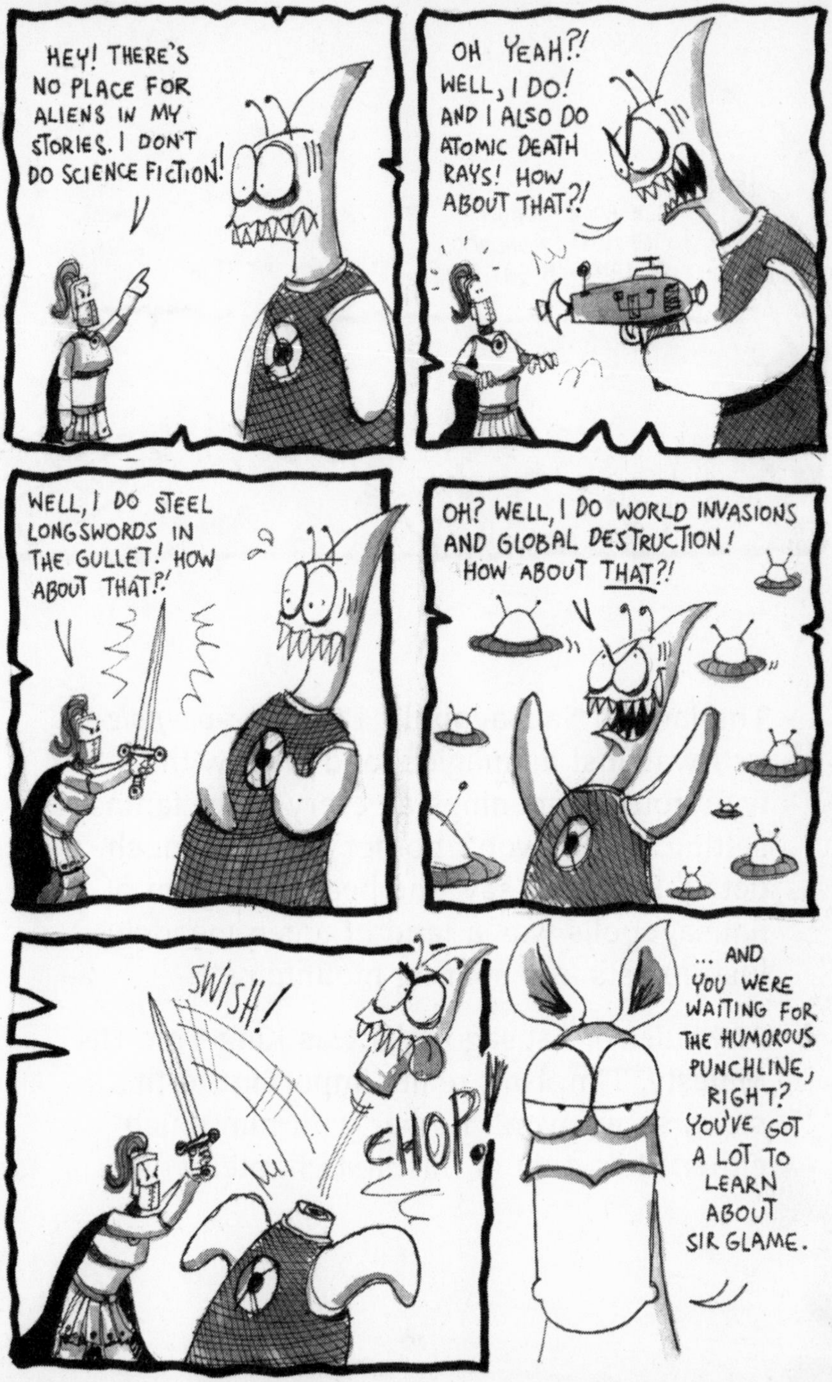
HEY! THERE'S NO PLACE FOR ALIENS IN MY STORIES. I DON'T DO SCIENCE FICTION!
OH YEAH?! WELL, I DO! AND I ALSO DO ATOMIC DEATH RAYS! HOW ABOUT THAT?!
WELL, I DO STEEL LONGSWORDS IN THE GULLET! HOW ABOUT THAT?!
OH? WELL, I DO WORLD INVASIONS AND GLOBAL DESTRUCTION! HOW ABOUT THAT?!
SWISH!
CHOP!
... AND YOU WERE WAITING FOR THE HUMOROUS PUNCHLINE, RIGHT? YOU'VE GOT A LOT TO LEARN ABOUT SIR GLAME.

The land of Sausagopolis ('*Sausage-op-pole-iss*') was just as magical and filled with wondrous happenings as every other fantasy setting, so we won't bother with too much detail. Let's just say 'the beautiful realm of Sausagopolis was a land of green meadows, lush forests and soaring mountains'.

The ruler of Sausagopolis was King Tim. His Majesty, Tim, isn't really important to this story, so we won't bother with him much either. He's only in this first chapter.

King Tim (being a wise ruler) always called on Sir Glame when he had problems. When a fire-breathing dragon was terrorising villagers to the north, Sir Glame went and slew it. When a mutated turtle was terrorising villagers to the south, Sir Glame went and slew that as well. When sharkmen from Neptune terrorised villagers in the east, you can bet he slew them. And when a villager's kitty was stuck up a tree in the west, he went and slew it too.

I AM ACTUALLY A VERY IMPORTANT CHARACTER. YOU'LL SEE...

KING TIM

ANOTHER PROBLEM SOLVED!

HERE LIES MR. SOX R.I.P.

Life in the far-off realm was better for everyone with Sir Glame around. Folk knew that if trouble arose they had a hero to turn to. And, right now, Sausagopolis was in desperate need of one.

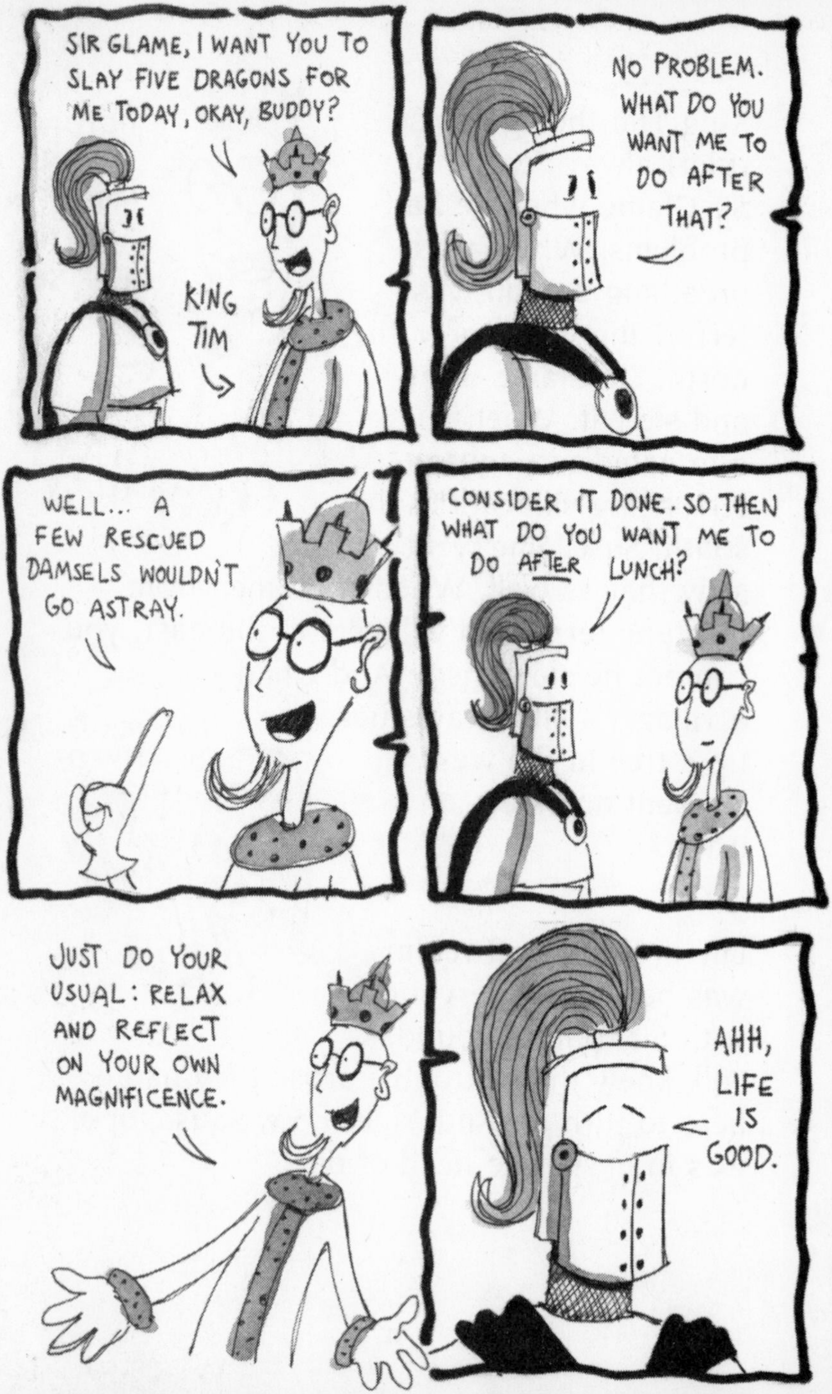
SIR GLAME, I WANT YOU TO SLAY FIVE DRAGONS FOR ME TODAY, OKAY, BUDDY?
KING TIM
NO PROBLEM. WHAT DO YOU WANT ME TO DO AFTER THAT?
WELL... A FEW RESCUED DAMSELS WOULDN'T GO ASTRAY.
CONSIDER IT DONE. SO THEN WHAT DO YOU WANT ME TO DO AFTER LUNCH?
JUST DO YOUR USUAL: RELAX AND REFLECT ON YOUR OWN MAGNIFICENCE.
AHH, LIFE IS GOOD.

KING TIM'S MORNING EXERCISE...

THESE WALKS WOULD BE A LOT MORE FUN IF I DIDN'T HAVE TO DO THEM.

The strife began a week ago. One sunny morning King Tim happened to be strolling through his palace when he discovered a strange parcel on his front steps. Inside was a book – a dire, insidious book that would soon become the bane of Sausagopolis. Its title?

Saucy McRascal's Big Book of Fun!

When King Tim read the first few pages, he was horrified. The book was filled with rude, bawdy, lowbrow, off-colour poetry. It was the kind of poetry only the naughtiest child from the lousiest school, with the most irresponsible parents and the worst upbringing would write. Stuff only the most puerile, immature mind would think was funny. Clearly this Saucy McRascal was a horrible,

LUCKY I'M BALD ALREADY OR MY HAIR WOULD FALL OUT FROM SHOCK!

BIG BOOK OF F

horrible person.

The great trouble was that **Saucy McRascal's Big Book of Fun!** didn't just appear on the King's steps. It was mysteriously delivered to every household in Sausagopolis. Soon the streets rang with howls of disgust or fits of laughter. Children laughed the loudest, but concerned grown-ups soon pulled it from their hands and tossed the filthy tome into the fireplace. Yet once the rhymes were read, they could not be forgotten. Disobedient children and irresponsible grown-ups began saying them out loud in public places. The once magical land of Sausagopolis was now ringing with the vulgar verses of the slimy stranger, Saucy McRascal.

The mystery deepened when a note in black writing was found on the palace gates:

Let it be known that the once sweet Sausagopolis will soon be no more. Now all its soft-hearted citizens shall suffer under the offensive might of my bawdy verses. A horrible curse I place upon your land: **The Curse of the Saucy Scribblings!**
Regards,
The Mysterious McRascal

King Tim immediately called Sir Glame. 'You've got to help us!' he pleaded. 'We can't have our innocent storybook land destroyed by this filth!' Tim opened the vile volume and read:

> 'There once was a young girl called Lottie
>> Whose nose was all stuffed up and snotty
>>> She needed no tissue
>>>> Picking presented no issue
>>>>> She'd practised so much
>>>>>> On her botty.'

'Good Gravy!' said Sir Glame. 'How hideous! We can't have our citizens reading such offensive muck. I must protect them or who knows where it could lead! If they're reading rude poems today, by tomorrow they'll be joining street gangs and vandalising letterboxes!'

'We must act before it's too late,' agreed King Tim. 'Young minds are being warped even as we speak. Search the entire land and find this evildoer! This curse must be broken!'

Sir Glame saluted. 'Don't worry, Your Majesty. I'll protect our morals and decency. I won't rest until I've hacked Saucy McRascal limb from limb!'

King Tim gave him a big kiss on the forehead for luck and sent him on his way.

*   *   *

Bill was saddled up and waiting as Sir Glame marched out to the palace courtyard.

'So, noble steed? Are you ready for another daring and possibly deadly adventure into the darkest folds of Sausagopolis?'

Bill sighed. 'Glame, we need to talk...'

'That's the spirit!' Sir Glame leapt on Bill's back. 'I knew you'd be eager!'

They trotted through the palace gates. The quest had begun!

Aren't you excited, young reader? Yes, of course you are. This book is very interesting and better than most, so if you're not, it's your own fault. Remember, if you stop reading now, you're going to miss out on the surprise ending with giant, killer robots from hell that will blow your mind!

A Sir Glame & Bill Mini-Adventure
POINTLESS DISTRACTIONS

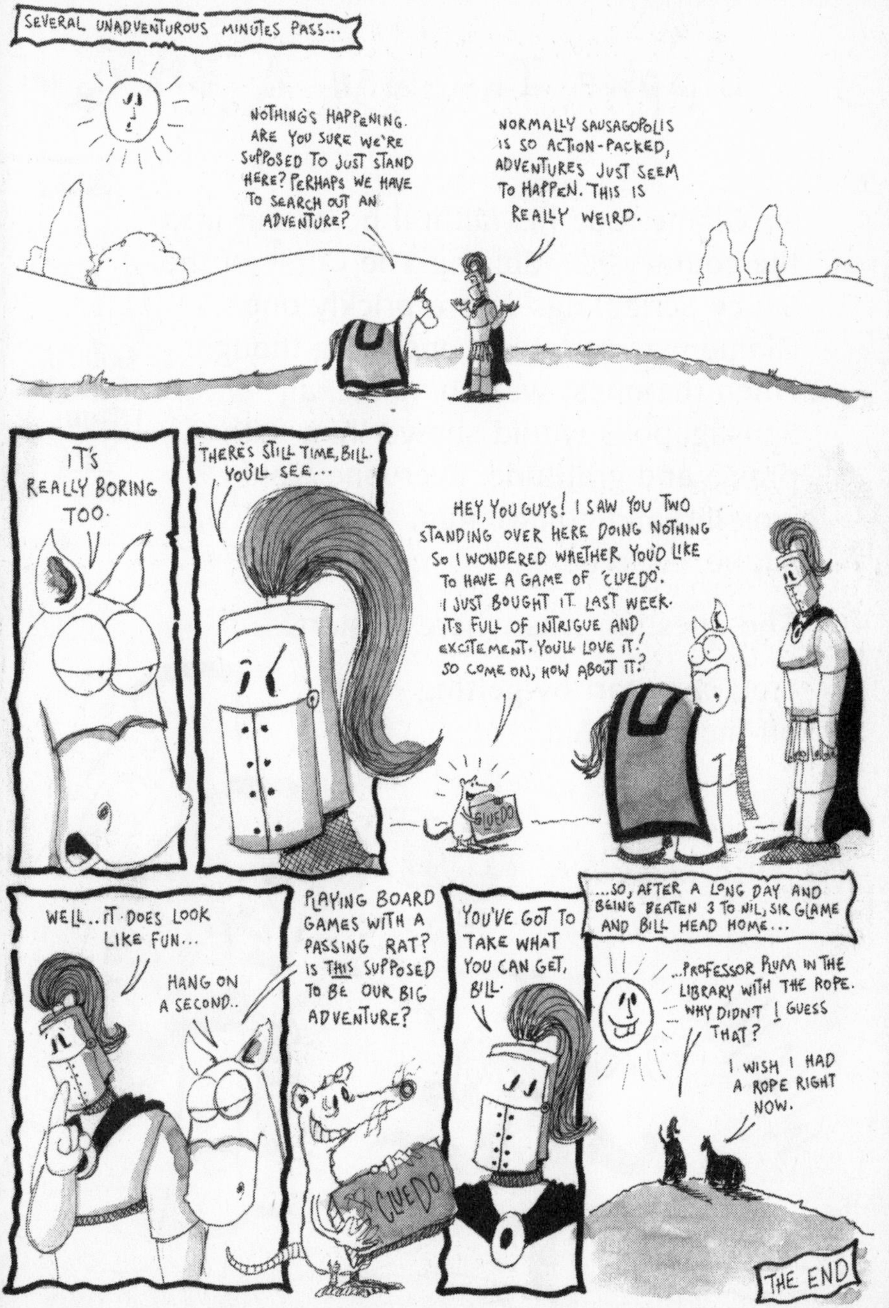
SEVERAL UNADVENTUROUS MINUTES PASS...
NOTHING'S HAPPENING. ARE YOU SURE WE'RE SUPPOSED TO JUST STAND HERE? PERHAPS WE HAVE TO SEARCH OUT AN ADVENTURE?
NORMALLY SAUSAGOPOLIS IS SO ACTION-PACKED, ADVENTURES JUST SEEM TO HAPPEN. THIS IS REALLY WEIRD.
IT'S REALLY BORING TOO.
THERE'S STILL TIME, BILL. YOU'LL SEE...
HEY, YOU GUYS! I SAW YOU TWO STANDING OVER HERE DOING NOTHING SO I WONDERED WHETHER YOU'D LIKE TO HAVE A GAME OF 'CLUEDO'. I JUST BOUGHT IT LAST WEEK. IT'S FULL OF INTRIGUE AND EXCITEMENT. YOU'LL LOVE IT! SO COME ON, HOW ABOUT IT?
CLUEDO
WELL.. IT DOES LOOK LIKE FUN...
HANG ON A SECOND..
PLAYING BOARD GAMES WITH A PASSING RAT? IS THIS SUPPOSED TO BE OUR BIG ADVENTURE?
CLUEDO
YOU'VE GOT TO TAKE WHAT YOU CAN GET, BILL.
...SO, AFTER A LONG DAY AND BEING BEATEN 3 TO NIL, SIR GLAME AND BILL HEAD HOME...
...PROFESSOR PLUM IN THE LIBRARY WITH THE ROPE. WHY DIDN'T I GUESS THAT?
I WISH I HAD A ROPE RIGHT NOW.
THE END

Chapter Two And A Bit

Sir Glame rode his faithful horse out into the countryside. Solving The Curse of the Saucy Scribblings was a prickly one. Glame was certain of one thing though: when the quest was complete, all Sausagopolis would shower him with praise and gratitude. Everyone would worship and admire him, the way it was supposed to be.

"FAITHFUL HORSE?" I THINK NOT!

The question was where to start?

'You can start by getting off me!' said Bill.

....OFF TO AN ENCOURAGING START...

WHAM!

Bill didn't like to be ridden. If Glame wanted to wear all that armour, let him be the one to carry it.

'If you ask me,' said Bill, 'this whole quest thing is a waste of time. I'm not worried. I think McRascal is quite the wordsmith. I enjoy his poems. Just listen to this one.' He flipped open his own copy of the **Big Book of Fun**...

> 'There was a little man
> With a little pair of pants
> And such a pair they were
> Through town in them he'd prance
>
> He strutted down the high street
> Sure he looked so smart
> Until the pants burst open
> When he let rip a giant –'

'That's quite enough!' Sir Glame declared. 'My ears are burning just listening to that gutter trash! Shame on you, Bill!'

I GUESS I SHOULDN'T HAVE EATEN ALL THOSE BEANS...

23

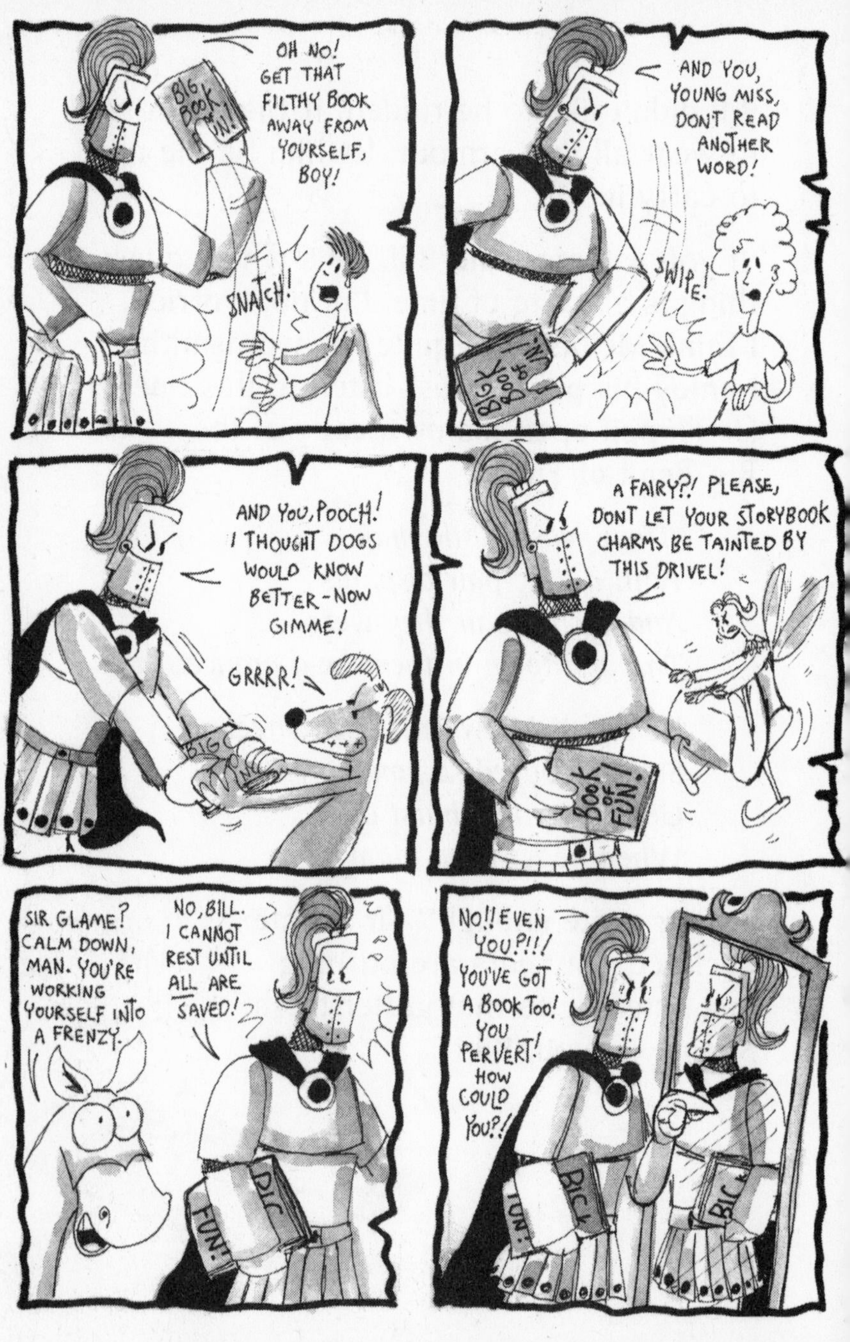
OH NO! GET THAT FILTHY BOOK AWAY FROM YOURSELF, BOY!
BIG BOOK OF FUN!
SNATCH!
AND YOU, YOUNG MISS, DONT READ ANOTHER WORD!
SWIPE!
AND YOU, POOCH! I THOUGHT DOGS WOULD KNOW BETTER - NOW GIMME!
GRRRR!
A FAIRY?! PLEASE, DONT LET YOUR STORYBOOK CHARMS BE TAINTED BY THIS DRIVEL!
BOOK OF FUN!
SIR GLAME? CALM DOWN, MAN. YOU'RE WORKING YOURSELF INTO A FRENZY.
NO, BILL. I CANNOT REST UNTIL ALL ARE SAVED!
NO!! EVEN YOU?!!! YOU'VE GOT A BOOK TOO! YOU PERVERT! HOW COULD YOU?!

'I don't care what you think.' Bill stashed away his book. 'I'll read more when you're not looking.'

'Oh no, you're not allowed to read in the bathroom. Remember our rule?'
Bill thought about that for a second.

'Have you been watching me go to the toilet?'

'Umm…no?' Sir Glame swallowed.

The two heroes searched the Great Forest, the Great Plains and the Great Desert of Sausagopolis. They found nothing.

'This is just great!' Bill growled. 'We've found nothing!'

'Now, now. Don't be like that. Saucy McRascal must be hiding somewhere. I'm sure we'll find something soon.' Glame was beginning to worry about his horse. They were supposed to be heroes. Bill seemed to be losing his noble spirit.

'I never had a noble spirit to begin with,' Bill frowned. 'It sounds made up.'

Glame sighed. 'That's enough, Bill. I'm just worried you're not being a team player. We're in this together, you know. I don't think you're motivated enough. You're not bringing anything to the table.'

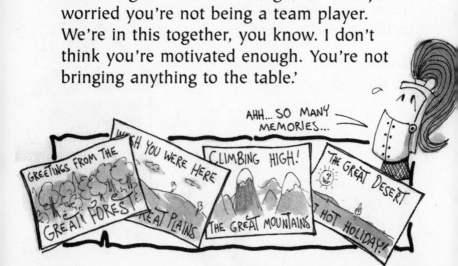

AHH... SO MANY MEMORIES...

GREETINGS FROM THE GREAT FOREST

WISH YOU WERE HERE GREAT PLAINS

CLIMBING HIGH! THE GREAT MOUNTAINS

THE GREAT DESERT HOT HOLIDAY!

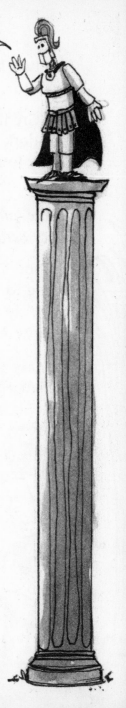

'What team?' said Bill. 'I'm just the horse. You're lucky I even show up for your dopey adventures. And what am I supposed to "bring to the table?" Let's just get this over with.'

Glame looked at him. 'I'm beginning to have issues with you, Bill.'

The two heroes decided to search the Great Swamp.

The Great Swamp was very, very swampy. And dark too. After much scouring, they finally found a clue – a note in black writing pinned to a tree:

All the land shall suffer under The Curse of the Saucy Scribblings! Bwah-ha-ha!

'Good Gravy!' said Glame. 'They even took time to write their deranged laughter. This is truly evil at work.'

'That's nothing,' said Bill.
'Take a look at *this*.'

Pinned to the next tree was another note.

And in case your wondering, I wrote the last note. The White Ferret.

'Well done, Bill! The villain has spelled it y-o-u-r instead of the correct y-o-u-'-r-e. That's a clue and a half!'

'Not that bit, genius. Look at the signature – and hey! Look at *this*.' Bill spotted something pinned to the next tree. It was a photo of a little white ferret writing the previous note. In one corner were the words, '*Thinking of you, the White Ferret.*'

THE GREAT SWAMP

I PREFER TO HAND-WRITE MY HATE MAIL. IT'S THE PERSONAL TOUCH I LIKE.

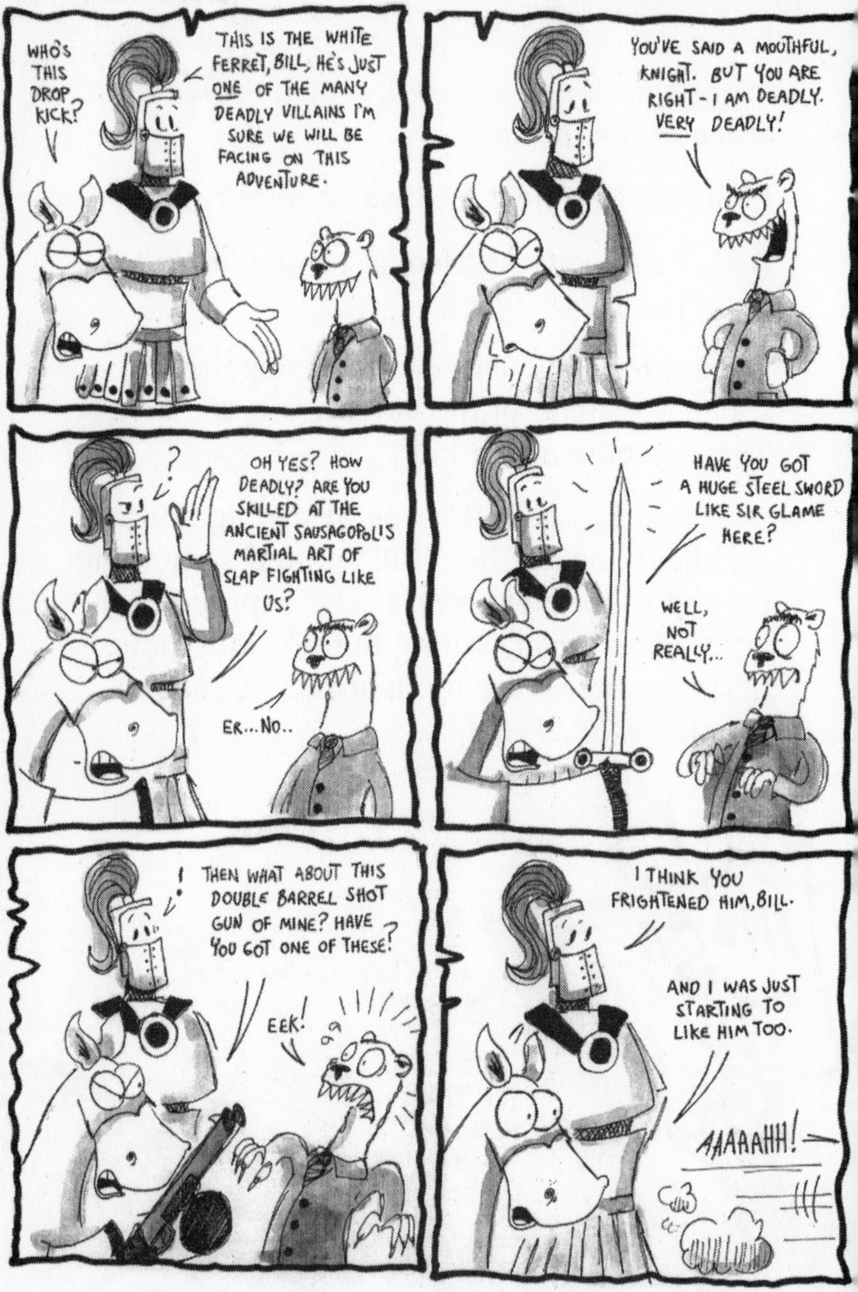
WHO'S THIS DROP KICK?
THIS IS THE WHITE FERRET, BILL, HE'S JUST ONE OF THE MANY DEADLY VILLAINS I'M SURE WE WILL BE FACING ON THIS ADVENTURE.
YOU'VE SAID A MOUTHFUL, KNIGHT. BUT YOU ARE RIGHT - I AM DEADLY. VERY DEADLY!
?
OH YES? HOW DEADLY? ARE YOU SKILLED AT THE ANCIENT SAUSAGOPOLIS MARTIAL ART OF SLAP FIGHTING LIKE US?
ER... NO..
HAVE YOU GOT A HUGE STEEL SWORD LIKE SIR GLAME HERE?
WELL, NOT REALLY...
!
THEN WHAT ABOUT THIS DOUBLE BARREL SHOT GUN OF MINE? HAVE YOU GOT ONE OF THESE?
EEK!
I THINK YOU FRIGHTENED HIM, BILL.
AND I WAS JUST STARTING TO LIKE HIM TOO.
AAAAAHH!

Glame's eyebrows shot up. 'Good Gravy! What do you think it all means?'

Suddenly a shrill voice rang out.

'Yooo-hooo! Over here!'

It was the White Ferret! Our two heroes quickly gave chase!

The White Ferret laughed madly and darted through the swamp. 'Run, run as fast as you can bear it! You can't catch me, I'm the White Ferret!'

'He's rhyming, Bill! He must be in league with that mysterious fiend, Saucy McRascal!'

Sir Glame and Bill chased the White Ferret through the swamp. Finally they cornered him in its deepest, darkest...umm...corner. There they discovered something majorly freaky.

Behind the White Ferret was a huge swirling vortex. One just like in those science-fiction movies, with flashing colours and wind and that deep 'woooor-woooor-woooor' sound.

WOOR
WOOR
WOOR

'Pretty impressive, huh?' the White Ferret boasted. 'I bet you've never seen a real inter-dimensional vortex before!'

WOOF
WOOF
WOOF

'What is it?' Sir Glame gasped.

Bill frowned. 'Pay attention to the narrative, Glame. He just told you: it's an inter-dimensional vortex!'

The White Ferret nodded. 'This is the mystical gateway to my master's domain. The one who wrote that cool book to curse Sausagopolis.'

'I think "curse" is a bit of an over-statement,' said Bill. 'I'd say it's more just a passing fad.'

The White Ferret ignored him and leapt into the vortex. In a blinding flash, he vanished.

'He left in rather a hurry,' said Glame.

'Anyway, what's a bizarre scientific oddity like that doing in our enchanted land, Bill? Someone's going to have to go in there and see what's on the other side.'

Bill said nothing.

Neither did Sir Glame.

'Well,' Bill shrugged finally. 'In the spirit of teamwork and participation, I've decided to bring something to the table: *You* go in there first.'

Sir Glame thought about it.

'Well . . . only if you come right after me, Bill. I'm worried about your enthusiasm. I've noticed you've been less than perky so far. Perhaps we should take time-out and have a performance discussion? I think you need to reapply yourself.'

Bill groaned. 'Okay, okay, I'll follow you. But this whole thing is just a big copy of *Alice in Wonderland*. You know, when Alice followed the White Rabbit down the rabbit hole?'

'Nonsense, Bill. It's nothing like that. This is a completely new and creative story. Not some cheap, second-rate rip-off. Now stop complaining and follow me!'

And so our two heroes jumped into the swirling vortex. In an instant, the knight and his horse were zapped to the darkest, dingiest and possibly spookiest corner of Sausagopolis.

YOU KNOW ALL THOSE STORIES THAT TELL YOU YOU'VE GOT TO TAKE RISKS IF YOU WANT TO SUCCEED? WELL, I'M LIVING PROOF THAT IS *BAD* ADVICE.

BUT YOU'RE NOT LIVING.

9

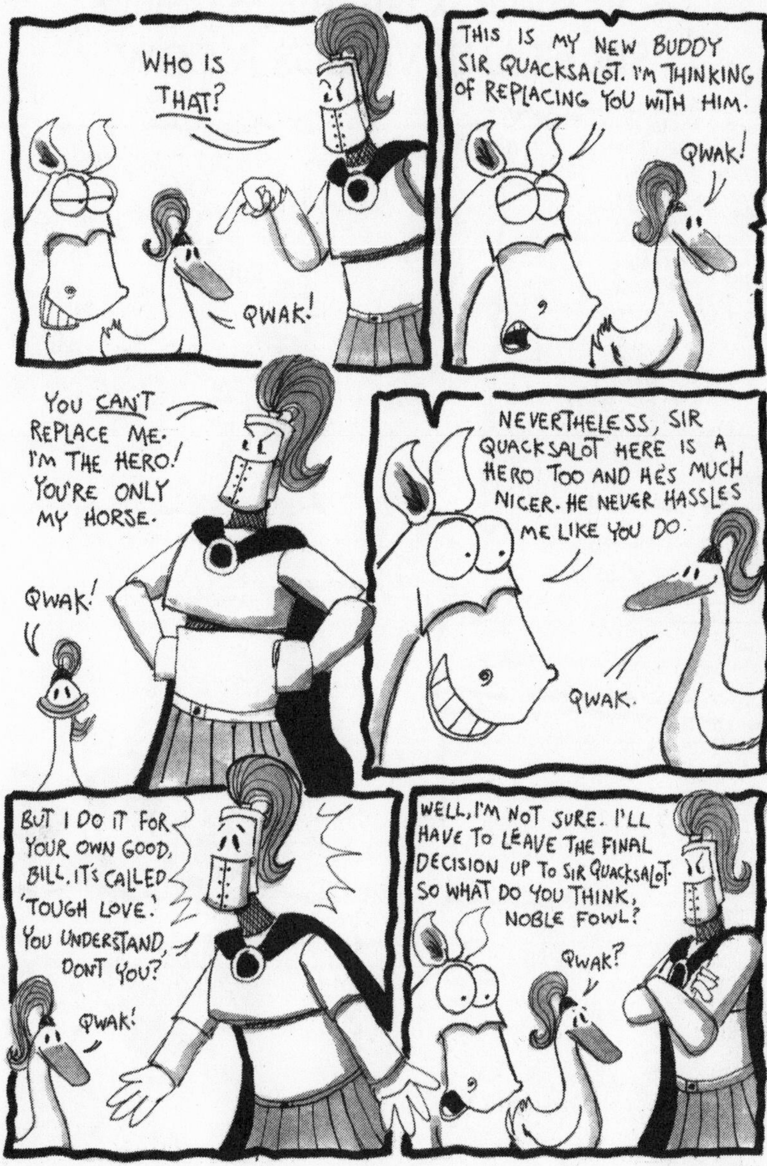

WHO IS THAT?
QWAK!
THIS IS MY NEW BUDDY SIR QUACKSALOT. I'M THINKING OF REPLACING YOU WITH HIM.
QWAK!
YOU CAN'T REPLACE ME. I'M THE HERO! YOU'RE ONLY MY HORSE.
QWAK!
NEVERTHELESS, SIR QUACKSALOT HERE IS A HERO TOO AND HE'S MUCH NICER. HE NEVER HASSLES ME LIKE YOU DO.
QWAK.
BUT I DO IT FOR YOUR OWN GOOD, BILL. IT'S CALLED 'TOUGH LOVE.' YOU UNDERSTAND, DONT YOU?
QWAK!
WELL, I'M NOT SURE. I'LL HAVE TO LEAVE THE FINAL DECISION UP TO SIR QUACKSALOT. SO WHAT DO YOU THINK, NOBLE FOWL?
QWAK?

A Sir Glame & Bill Mini-Adventure
SIR GLAME VERSUS A COW

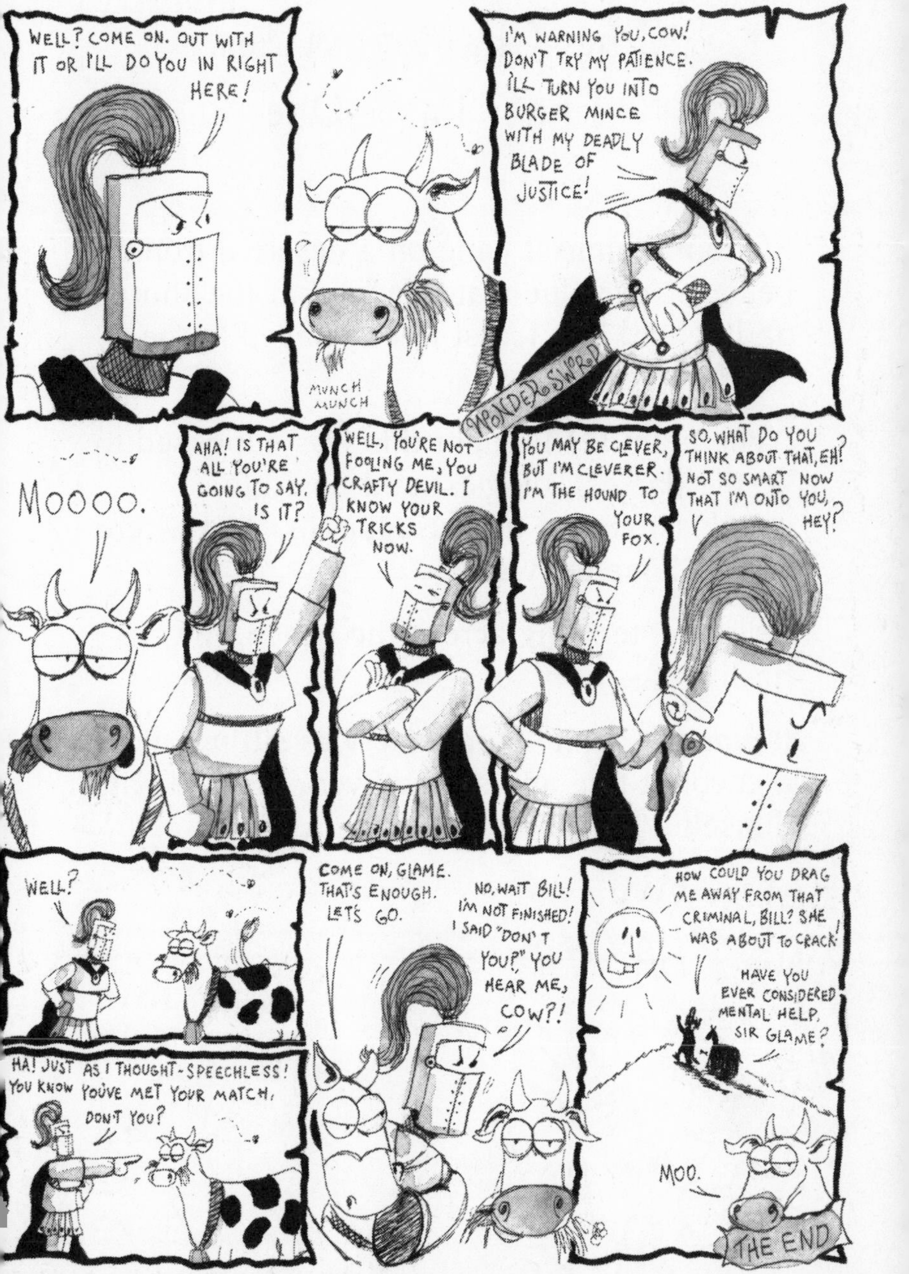

WELL? COME ON. OUT WITH IT OR I'LL DO YOU IN RIGHT HERE!
MUNCH MUNCH
I'M WARNING YOU, COW! DON'T TRY MY PATIENCE. I'LL TURN YOU INTO BURGER MINCE WITH MY DEADLY BLADE OF JUSTICE!
WONDER SWRD
MOOOO.
AHA! IS THAT ALL YOU'RE GOING TO SAY, IS IT?
WELL, YOU'RE NOT FOOLING ME, YOU CRAFTY DEVIL. I KNOW YOUR TRICKS NOW.
YOU MAY BE CLEVER, BUT I'M CLEVERER. I'M THE HOUND TO YOUR FOX.
SO, WHAT DO YOU THINK ABOUT THAT, EH? NOT SO SMART NOW THAT I'M ONTO YOU, HEY?
WELL?
HA! JUST AS I THOUGHT - SPEECHLESS! YOU KNOW YOU'VE MET YOUR MATCH, DON'T YOU?
COME ON, GLAME. THAT'S ENOUGH. LET'S GO.
NO, WAIT BILL! I'M NOT FINISHED! I SAID "DON'T YOU?" YOU HEAR ME, COW?!
HOW COULD YOU DRAG ME AWAY FROM THAT CRIMINAL, BILL? SHE WAS ABOUT TO CRACK!
HAVE YOU EVER CONSIDERED MENTAL HELP, SIR GLAME?
MOO.
THE END

The Chapter After
That Last One

Bill found himself lying on a deserted tropical beach. Clear blue water lapped at the shore and behind him forest trees swayed in the gentle breeze.

'Where am I? I thought this was supposed to be the darkest, dingiest and possibly spookiest corner of Sausagopolis. And where is Sir Glame anyway?'

Evil laughter rang across the beach. 'Bwah-ha-ha!'

It was the White Ferret! He was sitting under a coconut tree and seemed very pleased with himself.

HA! HA!
BWAH HA! HA!
HA! HA!
HA! HA!
HA!
HA!

GEE WHIZ! AND HERE
I THOUGHT IT WAS
IMPOSSIBLE TO OVER-
ACT IN A BOOK!

SHAKE
SHAKE

A TRAGEDY IN THE MAKING...

COME ON, COME TO PAPA...

'You fools!' he giggled. 'You shouldn't have followed me into the vortex. Now you'll *never* get home. You'll be trapped in this hell forever! Bwah-ha-ha!'

Bill looked around. 'It doesn't look much like hell to me. In fact, it looks quite lovely. I could get used to a place like this. And why did you say "fools" when I'm obviously alone?'

The White Ferret shrugged. 'Just for dramatic effect. Anyhow, since you are trapped here, I might as well reveal my master's whole devilishly dirty scheme – right after I enjoy a delicious coconut.'

The White Ferret shook the tree and a coconut fell out. It fell right on top of him – **CRUNCH!** – crushing his head completely. Bill went over. His body was still there, but his noggin was nothing but a squishy mess.

SUDDENLY I DON'T FEEL SO GOOD...

'Oh well.' Bill shrugged and ate his coconut. It was a little hard to chew, but he managed.

Now what was he going to do?

The horse lay on the beach and enjoyed the sun. It was so much more relaxing than going on some lame quest. He couldn't begin to guess which corner of Sausagopolis he'd been transported to. He decided to simply take it easy and have a snooze...

Zzzzzzzzzzzzzzzzzzzzzzzzzzzzzzzzzzzzzz...

...Suddenly Bill's eyes popped open. He was moving, but wasn't using his legs. He'd been tied up! Dozens of little fluffy creatures were around him, each a different colour from the next. They were carrying him through the forest.

'Hey?' he squirmed. 'What's going on?'

One of the tiny creatures climbed up on his nose. It was only as big as a tennis ball.

'Relax,' it said in a cute little voice. 'Wes is just takin' youse back to our village. Wes don't want youse cluttering up our beach.'

'But I was just having a snooze. What *are* you freaks anyway?'

WELL,
THIS IS
ODD...

'Wes is called Fuzzies. My name is Mama Fuzzy. I is the leader. Wes all live nearby. Wes tied you up sos you don't try and runs away from us. Wes found your friend too. The metal man. Wes gots him back at the village.'

Soon they arrived at a small clearing deep in the forest full of tiny houses carved out of mushrooms. Each had a little door and a little chimney. There were little roads and a little town square. In the middle of the square there was Sir Glame, tied up as well. The Fuzzies plonked Bill down beside the captured knight.

'Bill!' Sir Glame said, happy to see his friend. 'They got you too? I was washing my under-wear by the shore when they jumped me.'

'Why were you washing your underwear?'

Glame went red. '...Umm...I'll tell you later.'

The Fuzzies scurried about, talking in their own twee little language.

Bill looked around, annoyed. 'Will you get a load of this place? It's all so sweet and cute, I think I'm going to hurl. Look – they've even put curtains on their mailboxes!'

'I think it's delightful,' said Sir Glame. 'This is what Sausagopolis is *meant* to be about. I bet these little folks would never *dream* of reading a Saucy McRascal book.'

Mama Fuzzy came up to them.

'I hope youse two be happy here in Fuzzy Village.'

'You mean you're going to keep us here?' asked Glame.

'That's right,' Mama nodded. 'Wes going to keep youse here until tonight. Then wes going to sacrifice youse to our god and have a feast.'

'What?' Bill gasped. 'You mean you're going to *eat* us?'

'Ah-huh,' Mama smiled and blinked her big eyes. 'Wes bet youse is yummy.'

Bill and Glame looked at each other nervously. Glame leaned over and whispered to his horse.

'Quickly, Bill, distract them for a moment. I'm going to try something.'

GREAT
GOD OF
THE FUZZIES

YOU KNOW, IT
KIND OF LOOKS
LIKE YOUR
MOTHER.

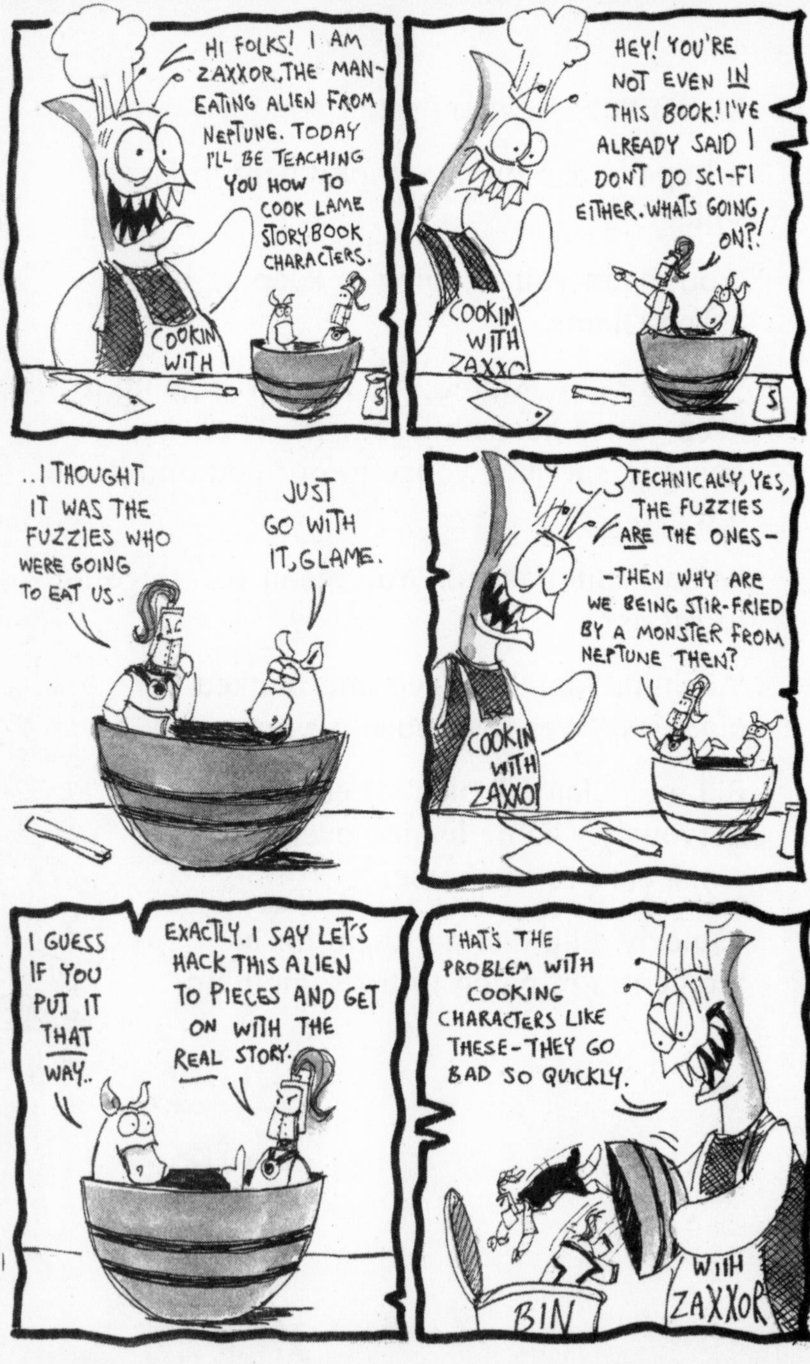
HI FOLKS! I AM ZAXXOR, THE MAN-EATING ALIEN FROM NEPTUNE. TODAY I'LL BE TEACHING YOU HOW TO COOK LAME STORYBOOK CHARACTERS.
COOKIN WITH
S
HEY! YOU'RE NOT EVEN IN THIS BOOK! I'VE ALREADY SAID I DON'T DO SCI-FI EITHER. WHATS GOING ON?!
COOKIN WITH ZAXXO
S
..I THOUGHT IT WAS THE FUZZIES WHO WERE GOING TO EAT US..
JUST GO WITH IT, GLAME.
TECHNICALLY, YES, THE FUZZIES ARE THE ONES-
-THEN WHY ARE WE BEING STIR-FRIED BY A MONSTER FROM NEPTUNE THEN?
COOKIN WITH ZAXXO
I GUESS IF YOU PUT IT THAT WAY..
EXACTLY. I SAY LET'S HACK THIS ALIEN TO PIECES AND GET ON WITH THE REAL STORY.
THAT'S THE PROBLEM WITH COOKING CHARACTERS LIKE THESE- THEY GO BAD SO QUICKLY.
BIN
WITH ZAXXOR

'Okay,' said Bill. He turned to Mama Fuzzy.
'Hey, all you little goofballs, I've got a story
I think you need to hear. It's about eating
things you shouldn't.'

'What be that?' Mama Fuzzy asked.

As Sir Glame worked his way out of the
ropes, Bill kept the Fuzzies' attention away
from him. 'It's called *The Lolly*,' he said.
'It's a little verse I remember,
penned by an unknown writer
called Saucy McRascal.
Ahem.

SOME SAY WE FUZZIES ARE A CHEAP COPY OFF THE EWOKS, BUT I PREFER TO THINK OF US AS A CHEAP COPY OFF THE SMURFS.

'I ate a big red lolly
It made me feel quite sorry
I found it in the gutter
I began to cough and splutter,
And I died a slow, hideous, gut-wrenching,
bowel-churning, agonising death for my folly.'

Bill smiled. The Fuzzies were white with horror.
They had never heard such an awful –

Suddenly Sir Glame was free! He jumped up
and drew his sword.

'Now's our chance, Bill! Destroy them!'

Before Bill could even move Sir Glame went to work. Like a chainsaw, he chopped into the Fuzzies, sending blood and guts all over the place. The little devils didn't know what had hit them. Then the noble knight ran around smashing all their little homes flat as pancakes. Soon there was nothing left of the Fuzzies and their village but a big gooey mess.

Bill rolled his eyes.

'Don't you think that was a bit...much?'

Sir Glame wiped the gore off his sword. 'What do you mean?'

'I mean you're supposed to be the good guy. I just got through telling them a supposedly "bad" Saucy McRascal poem, and then you go and hack them to bits!'

'Yes, you're right, Bill. It was wrong of you to torture them with that horrible poem.'

'But *you're* actually the one who's going around terrorising everyone!'

Glame shook his head. 'Evil comes in many forms, Bill. You'd be wise to remember that.'

Bill frowned. 'You're just lucky I get paid to be here.'

Glame's eyebrows shot up. 'You get *paid*?'

A Sir Glame & Bill Mini-Adventure
SIR GLAME VERSUS THE NATIONAL CHILDREN'S ADVISORY BOARD

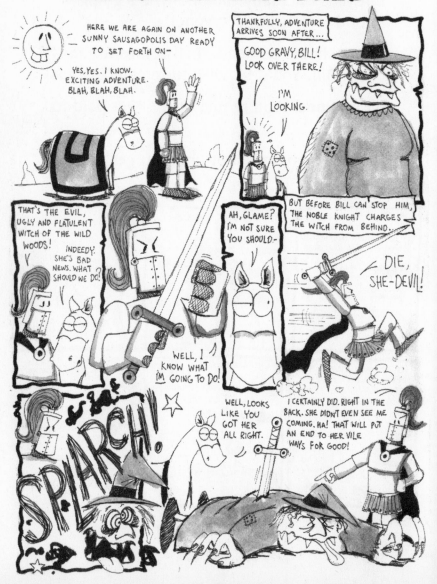

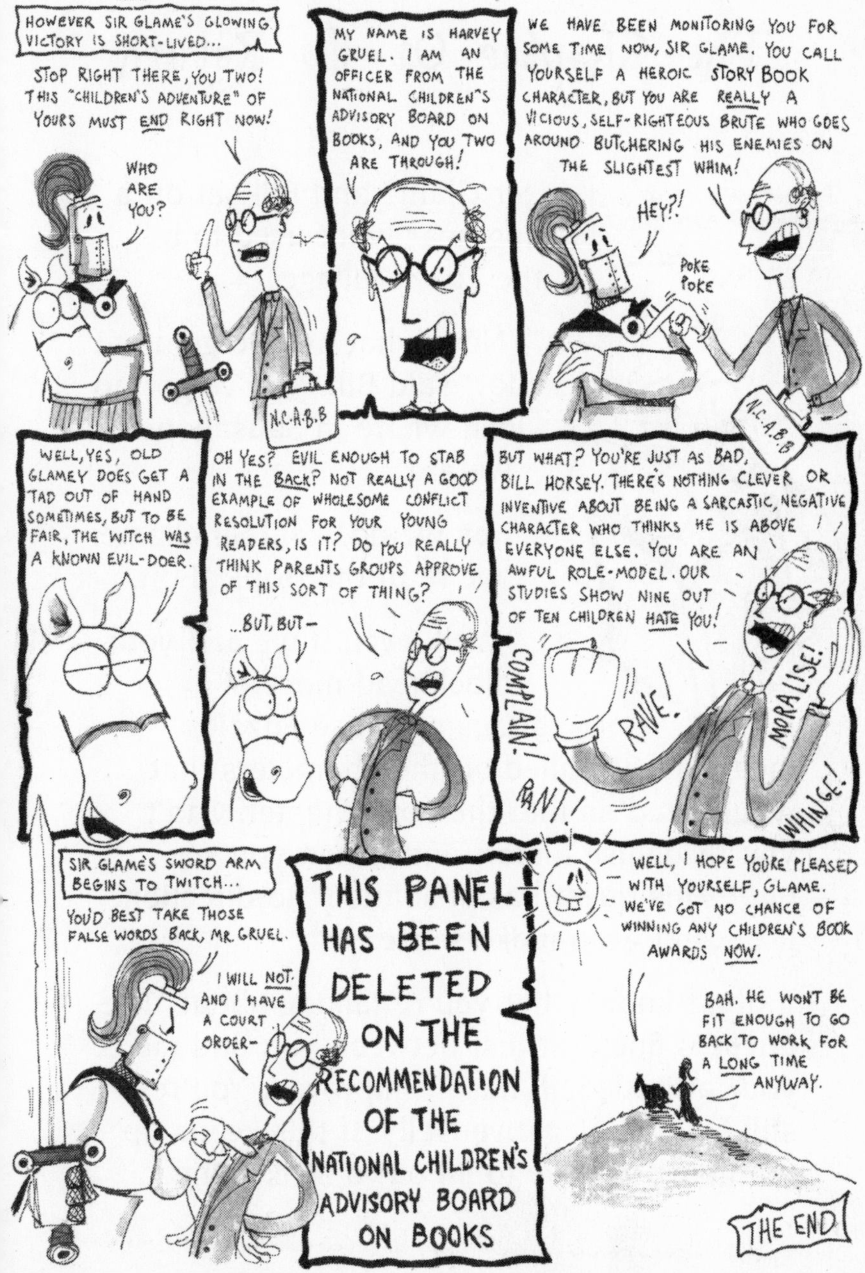

HOWEVER SIR GLAME'S GLOWING VICTORY IS SHORT-LIVED...
STOP RIGHT THERE, YOU TWO! THIS "CHILDREN'S ADVENTURE" OF YOURS MUST END RIGHT NOW!
WHO ARE YOU?
N.C.A.B.B
MY NAME IS HARVEY GRUEL. I AM AN OFFICER FROM THE NATIONAL CHILDREN'S ADVISORY BOARD ON BOOKS, AND YOU TWO ARE THROUGH!
WE HAVE BEEN MONITORING YOU FOR SOME TIME NOW, SIR GLAME. YOU CALL YOURSELF A HEROIC STORY BOOK CHARACTER, BUT YOU ARE REALLY A VICIOUS, SELF-RIGHTEOUS BRUTE WHO GOES AROUND BUTCHERING HIS ENEMIES ON THE SLIGHTEST WHIM!
HEY?!
POKE POKE
N.C.A.B.B
WELL, YES, OLD GLAMEY DOES GET A TAD OUT OF HAND SOMETIMES, BUT TO BE FAIR, THE WITCH WAS A KNOWN EVIL-DOER.
OH YES? EVIL ENOUGH TO STAB IN THE BACK? NOT REALLY A GOOD EXAMPLE OF WHOLESOME CONFLICT RESOLUTION FOR YOUR YOUNG READERS, IS IT? DO YOU REALLY THINK PARENTS GROUPS APPROVE OF THIS SORT OF THING?
...BUT, BUT-
BUT WHAT? YOU'RE JUST AS BAD, BILL HORSEY. THERE'S NOTHING CLEVER OR INVENTIVE ABOUT BEING A SARCASTIC, NEGATIVE CHARACTER WHO THINKS HE IS ABOVE EVERYONE ELSE. YOU ARE AN AWFUL ROLE-MODEL. OUR STUDIES SHOW NINE OUT OF TEN CHILDREN HATE YOU!
COMPLAIN!
RAVE!
MORALISE!
RANT!
WHINGE!
SIR GLAME'S SWORD ARM BEGINS TO TWITCH...
YOU'D BEST TAKE THOSE FALSE WORDS BACK, MR. GRUEL.
I WILL NOT. AND I HAVE A COURT ORDER-
THIS PANEL HAS BEEN DELETED ON THE RECOMMENDATION OF THE NATIONAL CHILDREN'S ADVISORY BOARD ON BOOKS
WELL, I HOPE YOU'RE PLEASED WITH YOURSELF, GLAME. WE'VE GOT NO CHANCE OF WINNING ANY CHILDREN'S BOOK AWARDS NOW.
BAH. HE WON'T BE FIT ENOUGH TO GO BACK TO WORK FOR A LONG TIME ANYWAY.
THE END

The Chapter Of No Return

PERHAPS WE SHOULD JUST SKIP AHEAD AND SEE WHAT WE ARE SUPPOSED TO DO NEXT

Sir Glame and Bill sat on a log near what used to be the Fuzzy village.

'Now what are we going to do?' said Bill. 'We've got no idea where in Sausagopolis we are.'

'Yes we do,' said Sir Glame, 'we're in the tropical bit.'

'Well, even if we are, your blockhead move of attacking those Fuzzies means we've killed off the characters that would lead us into the next chapter. Can't you recognise a story-link when you see one? This quest has absolutely no direction. It doesn't even make sense.'

'I don't know what you're talking about. The quest is fine. But just between you and me, your attitude still hasn't improved. You're still being a Negative Nelly. If this keeps up I'm going to have to fill out a Strike One disciplinary form and hand it in to the Palace. We must keep searching, that's all.'

'But searching is *all* we've been doing. It's boring. Can't we do something different?'

Bill was right. Just wandering around searching was as boring as...um...something really boring. With the Fuzzies gone, nothing short of a miracle (or a highly contrived plot twist) would get them out of this.

Suddenly Sir Glame stood up.

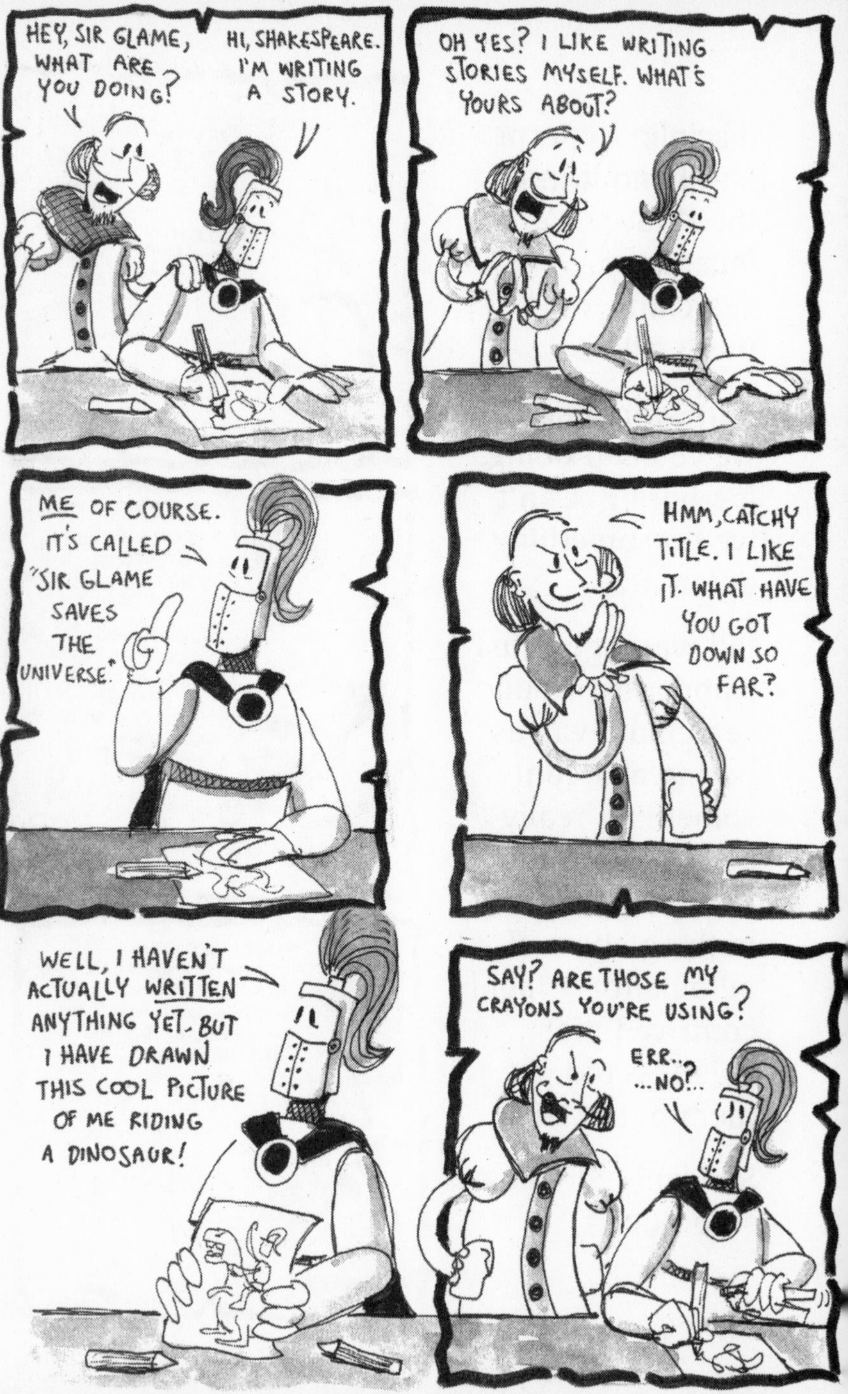
HEY, SIR GLAME, WHAT ARE YOU DOING?
HI, SHAKESPEARE. I'M WRITING A STORY.
OH YES? I LIKE WRITING STORIES MYSELF. WHAT'S YOURS ABOUT?
ME OF COURSE. IT'S CALLED "SIR GLAME SAVES THE UNIVERSE."
HMM, CATCHY TITLE. I LIKE IT. WHAT HAVE YOU GOT DOWN SO FAR?
WELL, I HAVEN'T ACTUALLY WRITTEN ANYTHING YET. BUT I HAVE DRAWN THIS COOL PICTURE OF ME RIDING A DINOSAUR!
SAY? ARE THOSE MY CRAYONS YOU'RE USING?
ERR.. ...NO?..

'Hey, Bill, look at this!' Glame walked over to a nearby bush. Brushing its leaves aside, he found a signpost. In big black letters it read: *For a good time come to Saucy McRascal's.* Underneath was an arrow pointing further inland.

'See?' Glame clapped his hands. 'We'll just follow this arrow.'

'Yes,' Bill said. 'What a strange and unlikely stroke of luck.' It was incredibly hard to believe, but it was good enough for him.

A Sir Glame & Bill Mini-Adventure
SIR GLAME'S HERO SANDWICH

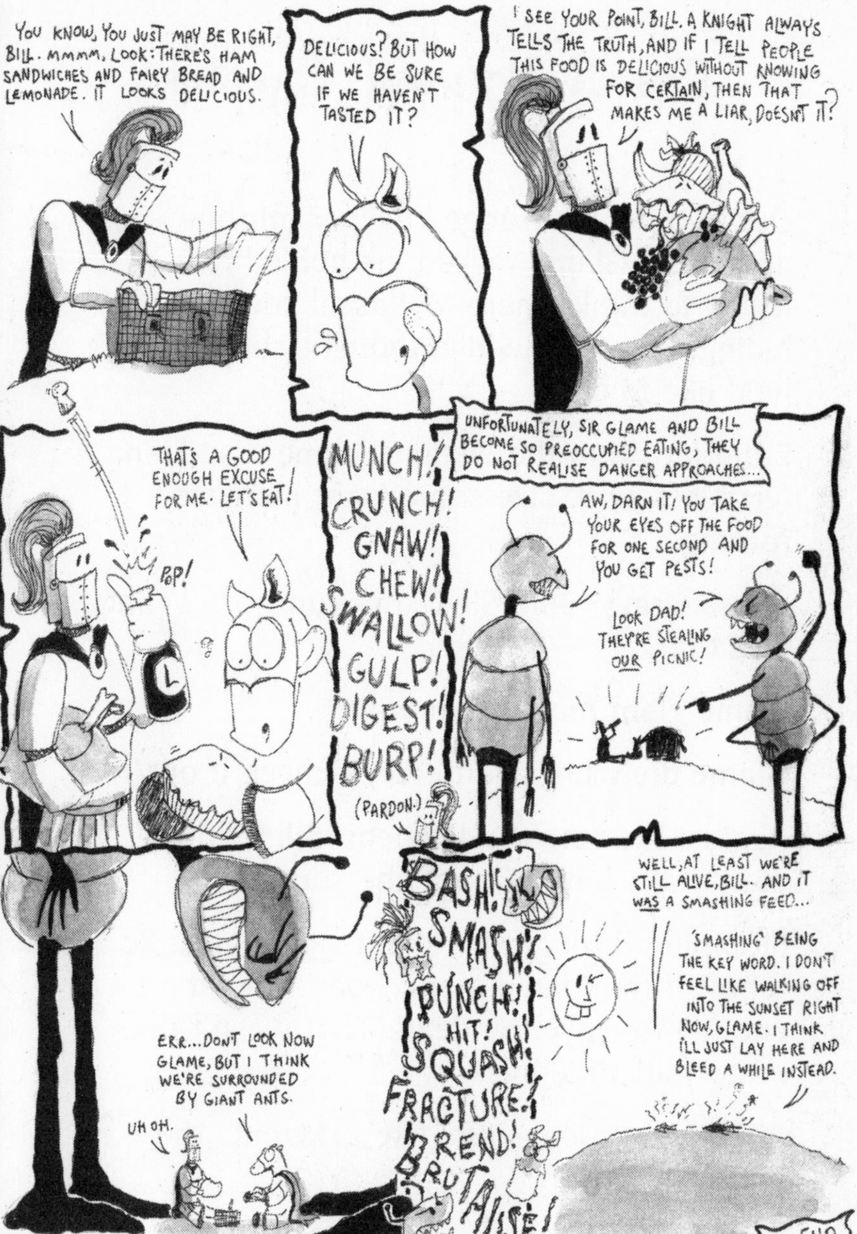

YOU KNOW, YOU JUST MAY BE RIGHT, BILL. MMMM, LOOK: THERE'S HAM SANDWICHES AND FAIRY BREAD AND LEMONADE. IT LOOKS DELICIOUS.
DELICIOUS? BUT HOW CAN WE BE SURE IF WE HAVEN'T TASTED IT?
I SEE YOUR POINT, BILL. A KNIGHT ALWAYS TELLS THE TRUTH, AND IF I TELL PEOPLE THIS FOOD IS DELICIOUS WITHOUT KNOWING FOR CERTAIN, THEN THAT MAKES ME A LIAR, DOESN'T IT?
THAT'S A GOOD ENOUGH EXCUSE FOR ME. LET'S EAT!
POP!
L
MUNCH! CRUNCH! GNAW! CHEW! SWALLOW! GULP! DIGEST! BURP!
(PARDON.)
UNFORTUNATELY, SIR GLAME AND BILL BECOME SO PREOCCUPIED EATING, THEY DO NOT REALISE DANGER APPROACHES...
AW, DARN IT! YOU TAKE YOUR EYES OFF THE FOOD FOR ONE SECOND AND YOU GET PESTS!
LOOK DAD! THEY'RE STEALING OUR PICNIC!
ERR...DONT LOOK NOW GLAME, BUT I THINK WE'RE SURROUNDED BY GIANT ANTS.
UH OH.
BASH! SMASH! PUNCH! HIT! SQUASH! FRACTURE! REND! BRUTALISE!
WELL, AT LEAST WE'RE STILL ALIVE, BILL. AND IT WAS A SMASHING FEED...
'SMASHING' BEING THE KEY WORD. I DON'T FEEL LIKE WALKING OFF INTO THE SUNSET RIGHT NOW, GLAME. I THINK I'LL JUST LAY HERE AND BLEED A WHILE INSTEAD.
THE END.

The Hollywood Chapter

Our two heroes trudged deeper into the jungle. Sir Glame racked his noble brain trying to think where McRascal could be hiding. Bill, meanwhile, thought about cakes he'd like to eat.

From far off in the distance came a sudden, terrible sound. Like some giant monster roaring.

'Good Gravy, Bill!' Sir Glame jumped. 'What was that?'

'Some giant monster roaring?'

Glame drew his sword. 'Let's check it out.'

Against his better judgement, Bill followed. It didn't take long to trace the sound.

Stomping through the forest was a gigantic robot! It thundered along, roaring loud enough to wake the dead. That wasn't the scary part though.

Bill cried, 'It looks just like...Winnie the Pooh!'

Sir Glame gasped. 'It's coming straight for us!'

The knight knew he had to do something. Waving his sword, he ran at the giant metal bear and chopped into its leg. Sparks flew as the leg flew off its hinges. The giant beast collapsed onto the ground.

'Well, Sir Glame,' Bill sighed. 'I hope you're proud of yourself. You just killed Winnie the Pooh.'

'I never realised he was so big in real life.' The knight scratched his head.

'Cut! Cut! Cut!' came a voice. Bill turned to see a whole bunch of people with cameras, lighting and equipment set up behind him. A small man in a director's chair held a megaphone to his mouth. 'Who are you people? What do you think you're doing?'

'I just saved you from this robotic fiend, that's what!' said Sir Glame.

'No, no, no! You've just ruined my movie! Do you know how much that robot cost?' The man threw down the megaphone. 'That's it! I quit!' And he stormed off the set in disgust. Sir Glame and Bill just stood there. Two large men approached.

'Mr Hector would like to see you clowns in his office,' one said in a do-as-I-ask-or-we'll-break-your-fingers kind of way. 'Follow us.'

THE DREAM FACTORY

The two men led them to a swanky caravan parked behind all the cameras and equipment. Big gold letters on the side read: *HECTOR PICTURES*. The two men pushed Sir Glame and Bill through the door.

Sitting at his desk, smoking a cigar and looking very angry was Mr Hector.

'Do you two boys realise you've just lost me the best director in the business? It took millions to get Kay Fu Yung to work for me! I hope you've got a heck of a good reason for what you just did.'

But all Sir Glame and Bill could do was stare.

Finally Glame answered. 'I'm sorry, Mr Hector. We just weren't expecting you to be...a...'

'Yes, yes, I know,' Hector puffed. 'You weren't expecting me to be a half-eaten cheese, tomato and onion roll. I get that all the time. What do you think H.E.C.T.O.R. stands for? The movie business is tough, boys, there's not much room for minorities any more.'

MR HECTOR

'I didn't think they made movies in Sausagopolis,' Sir Glame said. 'I thought we were strictly a storybook, fantasy-type setting.'

Mr Hector snorted. 'Son, what you don't know about Sausagopolis I could choke a whale with. You just don't understand what I'm trying to create here, do you?'

Bill nodded. 'I do, Mr Hector.'

'No, I don't think you do, kid. You've just ruined my picture two days before we were due to finish. *Poohzilla* was going to be a blockbuster. Now it's all over.' The half-eaten roll sighed and took another puff of his cigar. He looked at Sir Glame. Suddenly a glimmer came to his eyes. 'Unless...how tall are you, steel-britches?'

'Who, me?'

Mr Hector smiled. 'Yeah, you'll do fine...'

* * *

Bill sat down in the director's chair and picked up the megaphone. 'Okay, everyone, quiet on set. Mr Hector trusted us to finish this film and by golly we're going to. Okay: lights...camera...action!'

Sir Glame thumped through the forest in his armour, wearing the giant steel Winnie-the-Pooh mask on his head. He roared as best he could.

'Okay, that's good Glame, good.' Bill directed him through his megaphone. 'You're angry.

Good. The aliens have hidden your "hunny" somewhere around here. You've got to find it. You're ready to tear the place apart if you don't. Roar. Roar like you're angry. Yes. You're so mad. Yes. That's it. Louder. Louder. No wait – CUT!'

Bill called Sir Glame over to his chair.

'What is it?' Glame panted.

'You're just not giving me enough energy, Glame. I need louder roars.'

'This whole thing is stupid.' Glame frowned.

'What are we doing making a movie anyway? We're meant to be solving The Curse of the Saucy Scribblings!'

'Hey, you're the one who got us into this mess. I'm just trying to help out Mr Hector.'

'But he's just a roll!'

'That's *enough* of your prejudices, Glame. Who's being the Negative Nelly now? Get back in there and give me all you've got.'

Sir Glame sighed and went back to work. It took Bill all afternoon to get the scene just right, but when they were done, it was worth it.

'So *now* we can leave?' Glame moaned.

'No, now I have to edit the film together. This is where I work my movie magic.'

I SIMPLY CANNOT WORK WITH THAT HORSE. HE AND I JUST HAVE TOO MANY CREATIVE DIFFERENCES. I'LL BE IN MY TRAILER.

Bill spent all night in the editing tent working on his creation. Sir Glame sat outside, annoyed. He decided to fill out a Strike One form. Bill was plainly using this movie to avoid their quest. King Tim would hear about this.

GLAMÈS FLASHY HOLLYWOOD ROBE.

When Bill was finished, everyone gathered in Mr Hector's caravan for the big premiere.

'I think you're really going to love it, Mr H,' Bill said, pleased with himself. 'It's the movie I was born to make.'

What followed were two hours unlike any Mr Hector had ever experienced. The film, now re-titled *FrankenPooh 3000*, was the most disturbing movie he'd ever seen. Filled with bombs, fights, guns, gore, mindless violence and blatant nudity, it was nothing like what he'd planned.

'Good Gravy, Bill,' Sir Glame sighed as the end credits rolled. 'What was all *that* about? You cut out all my best scenes!'

'I'll tell you what it's about!' Hector screamed. 'I'm ruined! What in the name of King Tim did you do? You took a beautiful story and warped it into horror! Are you insane?'

'Hey!' Bill said annoyed. 'This film is gold. It's got box office written all over it. It'll make millions. I'm just giving the people what they want – thrills, action, adventure!'

'That's not how you tell a story,' Hector said. 'It has to have *direction*. Good plot. Interesting characters, ones people can relate

to and care about. Deep characters that grow and learn and develop. You've just made a shallow, noisy mess that goes nowhere. Not to mention Sir Glame's limp performance as Pooh!'

68

'You just don't understand my vision,' Bill said in disgust. 'Come on, Glame. We're going. What does a half-eaten roll know about movie-making anyway?'

'You're right, Bill,' agreed Sir Glame. 'I thought my acting had a really fresh quality.'

So our two heroes left the set. Bill took his film with them.

'I wonder if George Lucas ever had these problems?'

'Who's George Lucas?' said Sir Glame.

Bill sighed. 'I wish *you* were in a galaxy far, far away.'

A Sir Glame & Bill Mini-Adventure
GLAME GETS CONFUSED (AGAIN)

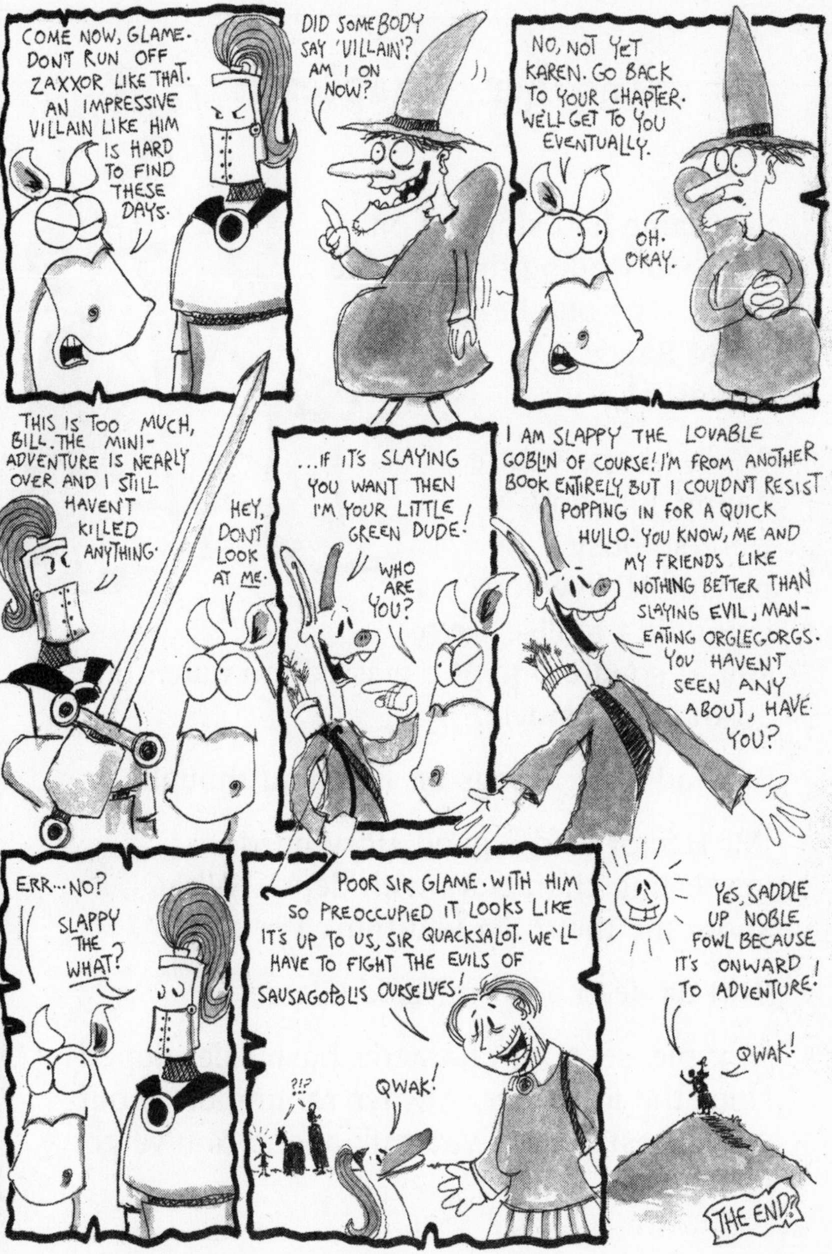
COME NOW, GLAME. DON'T RUN OFF ZAXXOR LIKE THAT. AN IMPRESSIVE VILLAIN LIKE HIM IS HARD TO FIND THESE DAYS.
DID SOMEBODY SAY 'VILLAIN'? AM I ON NOW?
NO, NOT YET KAREN. GO BACK TO YOUR CHAPTER. WE'LL GET TO YOU EVENTUALLY.
OH. OKAY.
THIS IS TOO MUCH, BILL. THE MINI-ADVENTURE IS NEARLY OVER AND I STILL HAVEN'T KILLED ANYTHING.
HEY, DONT LOOK AT ME.
...IF IT'S SLAYING YOU WANT THEN I'M YOUR LITTLE GREEN DUDE!
WHO ARE YOU?
I AM SLAPPY THE LOVABLE GOBLIN OF COURSE! I'M FROM ANOTHER BOOK ENTIRELY, BUT I COULDN'T RESIST POPPING IN FOR A QUICK HULLO. YOU KNOW, ME AND MY FRIENDS LIKE NOTHING BETTER THAN SLAYING EVIL, MAN-EATING ORGLEGORGS. YOU HAVEN'T SEEN ANY ABOUT, HAVE YOU?
ERR...NO?
SLAPPY THE WHAT?
POOR SIR GLAME. WITH HIM SO PREOCCUPIED IT LOOKS LIKE IT'S UP TO US, SIR QUACKSALOT. WE'LL HAVE TO FIGHT THE EVILS OF SAUSAGOPOLIS OURSELVES!
?!?
QWAK!
YES, SADDLE UP NOBLE FOWL BECAUSE IT'S ONWARD TO ADVENTURE!
QWAK!
THE END?

Another Chapter

Sir Glame had stopped on the road leading through the forest. The one he guessed led to Saucy McRascal.

'Well, I hope you're happy, Bill. You were so busy playing Hollywood you didn't realise we're still at square one. We wasted too much time on that silly movie.'

Bill had other things on his mind though.

'Mr Hector said a good story needs interesting characters with depth. What about me then? Do you think I'm deep?'

'Not as deep as I am,' said Glame.

'Oh, please. Your character hasn't developed since the first page. Always ranting on about your quest. It's all you talk about. You've got *no* depth.'

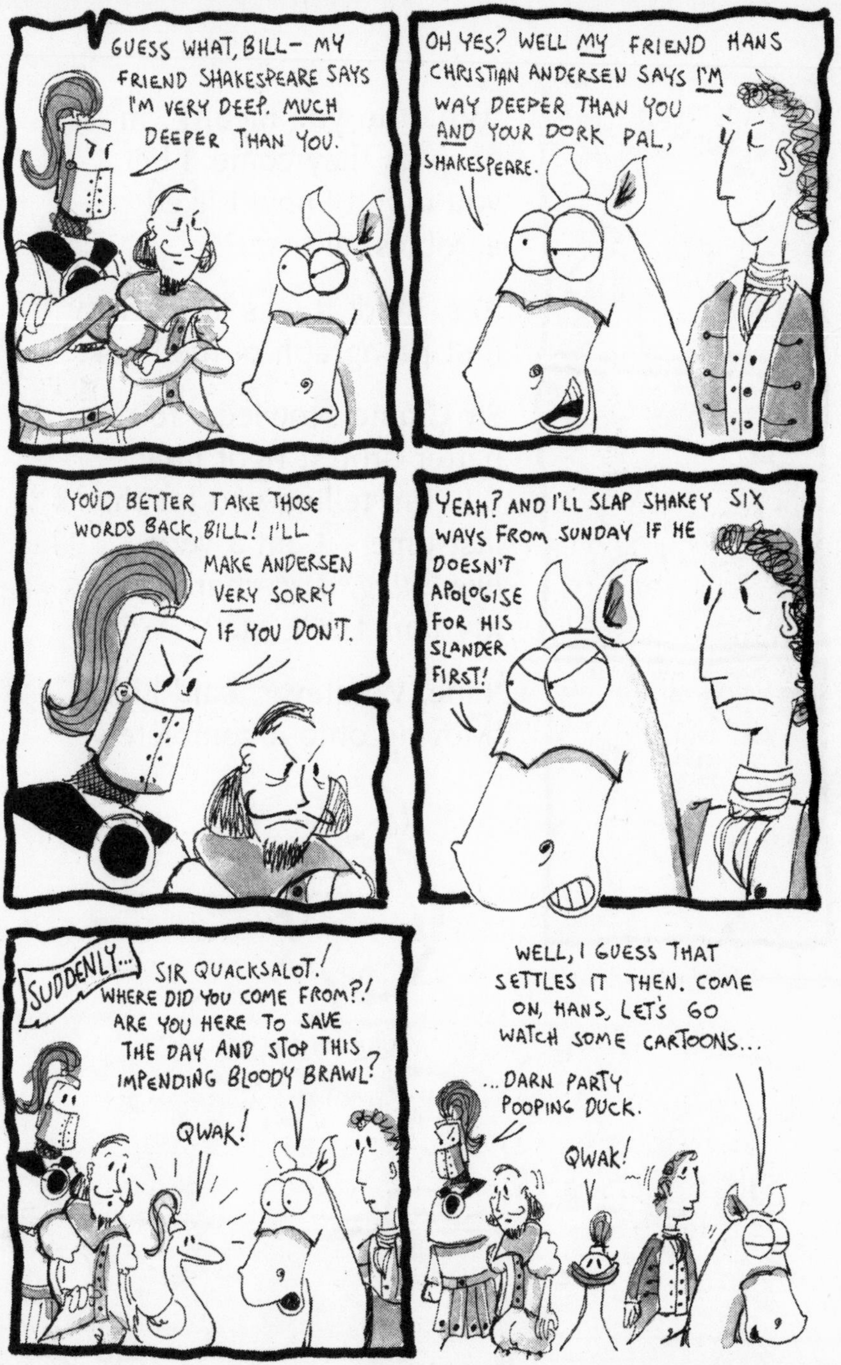
GUESS WHAT, BILL- MY FRIEND SHAKESPEARE SAYS I'M VERY DEEP. MUCH DEEPER THAN YOU.
OH YES? WELL MY FRIEND HANS CHRISTIAN ANDERSEN SAYS I'M WAY DEEPER THAN YOU AND YOUR DORK PAL, SHAKESPEARE.
YOU'D BETTER TAKE THOSE WORDS BACK, BILL! I'LL MAKE ANDERSEN VERY SORRY IF YOU DON'T.
YEAH? AND I'LL SLAP SHAKEY SIX WAYS FROM SUNDAY IF HE DOESN'T APOLOGISE FOR HIS SLANDER FIRST!
SUDDENLY...
SIR QUACKSALOT! WHERE DID YOU COME FROM?! ARE YOU HERE TO SAVE THE DAY AND STOP THIS IMPENDING BLOODY BRAWL?
QWAK!
WELL, I GUESS THAT SETTLES IT THEN. COME ON, HANS, LET'S GO WATCH SOME CARTOONS...
...DARN PARTY POOPING DUCK.
QWAK!

FUN & GAMES...

HEY, LET'S PLAY SIR GLAME. I HAVE ALL THE ACTION FIGURES.

COOL!

OH NO, WAIT. WE CAN'T. SIR GLAME'S BATTERIES HAVE GONE FLAT AGAIN.

WHAT DOES HE NEED BATTERIES FOR?

THEY POWER HIS MASSIVE EGO. I HAVE TO BUY NEW ONES ALL THE TIME.

I RECKON HE'S MORE FUN THIS WAY...

'What do you mean? I'm as deep as they come. I bet you didn't know I liked aerobics, did you?'

'Yes, I did. It was in the very first paragraph of the book.'

Sir Glame scowled. 'You'd better drop it right now, Bill. I'm telling you for the last time – I am a very *interesting, deep* character! My fans LOVE me!'

'Fine. Whatever,' said Bill. 'Moving onto a completely

A TRUCK IN SAUSAGOPOLIS? AND ON A COMPLETEY UNRELATED ISSUE, WHAT AM I DOING FLOATING UP HERE IN THIS CIRCLE?

different subject, I would have liked to taste Mr Hector. I've never eaten a movie producer who was a roll before.'

Sir Glame moaned. His horse wasn't even listening to him.

Suddenly the wheezing of an engine came from around the bend. Our two heroes jumped to one side as a truck chugged past them. It stopped down the road beside the busted-up robot Pooh. On the truck's side were the words: SAUSAGOPOLIS SCRAP.

Bill wondered, 'What's a truck doing in Sausagopolis? This is supposed to be a fantasy setting – no machines allowed.'

AT FIRST WHEN I WAS TOLD I WAS PICKING UP A TRUCKLOAD OF POO, I WAS A LITTLE PUT OFF...

Sir Glame nodded. 'I thought the same thing about the robot and all the movie cameras last chapter.'

A weird creature got out of the truck. A funky little mutant type thing. He carried a clipboard and started pawing through the wreckage, writing things down. When he'd finished, he picked up all the Pooh pieces and tossed them into his truck. Then he got in and drove away.

Bill looked at Sir Glame. 'What do you suppose that was about?'

'Isn't it obvious? *SAUSAGOPOLIS SCRAP* must have made the robot for Hector. They came to collect it. Didn't you see the invoice the mutant was writing up? That's a bill for the busted Pooh.'

The horse raised one eyebrow. 'You figured all that out just then?'

HEY, MAMA FUZZY, DON'T YOU THINK IT'S A BIT HARSH WE JUST GOT CASUALLY KILLED OFF DURING THE LAST FEW CHAPTERS?

I SURE DO. SUCH A FLIPPANT ATTITUDE TOWARDS DEATH CAN'T BE GOOD FOR THE EMOTIONAL WELL-BEING OF OUR YOUNGER READERS.

WELL, IF YOU TWO DON'T WANT YOUR GRAVES, I'LL TAKE ONE. MINE IS TOO LUMPY.

BEAT IT YOU SQUATTER.

'Of course, and that's not the half of it. The mutant's handwriting was the same evil black style as those notes we found in the Great Swamp.'

Bill frowned. 'Hey, wait a minute. How can you tell that? We were a good hundred feet away when the freak wrote up that invoice. Plus, we saw photos of the *White Ferret* writing those notes. Isn't it impossible for two people to have exactly the same writing?'

Sir Glame crossed his arms. 'Listen, if you're going to poke holes into everything I do, I'm not going to bring you on the next quest.'

'I'm not trying to be difficult, I'm just saying that, *one*: you can't possibly have figured all that out so easily, *two*: there's no chance you could read that invoice from way over here,

and *three*: it's impossible for two people to have exactly the same handwriting.'

Let's just stop here, shall we, young reader?

Okay, so Bill seems to have noticed some holes in the plot. For the sake of keeping things going, please ignore Bill and listen to Sir Glame. So what if he's figured everything out so quickly? He's a knight and is supposed to be clever. Bill just doesn't understand how to keep a story moving. That's why his *FrankenPooh 3000* movie was so bad. Now back to our heroes...

Sir Glame and Bill watched the truck speed off up the road.

Glame stamped his foot. 'We've got to go after that truck! I bet it'll lead us straight to the mystery supervillain!' He jumped on Bill's back. 'Let's go!'

Bill didn't move. 'Hey! You know I don't like to be ridden.'

'Aww, come on. I'll steal the truck and beat up the little mutant guy. Then we'll get answers!'

'Nope – no way!'

'Please?' Glame pleaded. 'What if I let you honk the horn as much as you want? I know how much you love to honk and shout at people.'

'Well...' Bill thought about it. '...okay.'

So the two heroes charged after the truck. Bill galloped along madly, the truck revving its engine to get away. When the mutant saw them in the rear-view mirror he skidded left and right. Bill dodged as Sir Glame drew his sword and slashed at the cab.

VARLET?

'Pull over, varlet!' he cried.
'I want words with you!'

Dust flew up from the truck's
wheels and the forest whipped
by with frightening speed. The
mutant made rude signals with
his fingers and drove
even faster.

'Did you see that, Bill? He's mocking us!
Get around in front of him. He'll swerve
and we'll run him off the road!'

Bill galloped harder. He was going so fast his
brain started to press against the back of his
skull. He jumped out in front of the truck.
Sir Glame held up his sword in triumph.
'Stop I say!'

HEY READERS! CHECK OUT
SIR QUACKSALOT'S AND MY OWN
MINI-ADVENTURE OVER THERE.
JUST TURN THE BOOK SIDE-
-WAYS AND ENJOY!

QWAK!

OH NO! AS IF I HAVEN'T
GOT ENOUGH PROBLEMS.
THERE WILL BE NO
SCENE-STEALING, GIMMICKY
'SIDEWAYS ADVENTURES'
IN MY BOOK!

SIDEWAYS ADVENTURE

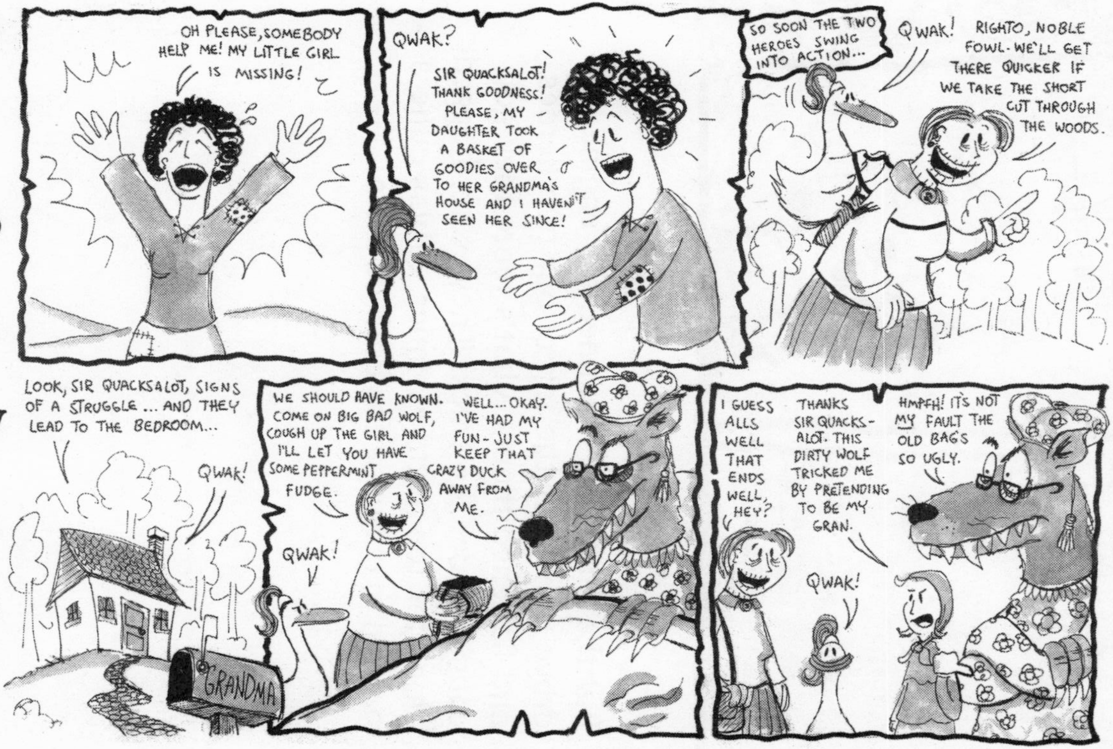
OH PLEASE, SOMEBODY HELP ME! MY LITTLE GIRL IS MISSING!
QWAK?
SIR QUACKSALOT! THANK GOODNESS! PLEASE, MY DAUGHTER TOOK A BASKET OF GOODIES OVER TO HER GRANDMA'S HOUSE AND I HAVEN'T SEEN HER SINCE!
SO SOON THE TWO HEROES SWING INTO ACTION...
QWAK!
RIGHTO, NOBLE FOWL- WE'LL GET THERE QUICKER IF WE TAKE THE SHORT CUT THROUGH THE WOODS.
LOOK, SIR QUACKSALOT, SIGNS OF A STRUGGLE ... AND THEY LEAD TO THE BEDROOM...
QWAK!
GRANDMA
WE SHOULD HAVE KNOWN. COME ON BIG BAD WOLF, COUGH UP THE GIRL AND I'LL LET YOU HAVE SOME PEPPERMINT FUDGE.
QWAK!
WELL... OKAY. I'VE HAD MY FUN- JUST KEEP THAT CRAZY DUCK AWAY FROM ME.
I GUESS ALLS WELL THAT ENDS WELL, HEY?
THANKS SIR QUACKSALOT. THIS DIRTY WOLF TRICKED ME BY PRETENDING TO BE MY GRAN.
QWAK!
HMPFH! IT'S NOT MY FAULT THE OLD BAG'S SO UGLY.

But the mutant just gunned the engine. He drove right over the top of our two heroes and flattened them. What's more they got caught under the truck. They were dragged along for the next few miles. It was quite a painful experience for both of them.

A Sir Glame & Bill Mini-Adventure
GONE FISHIN'

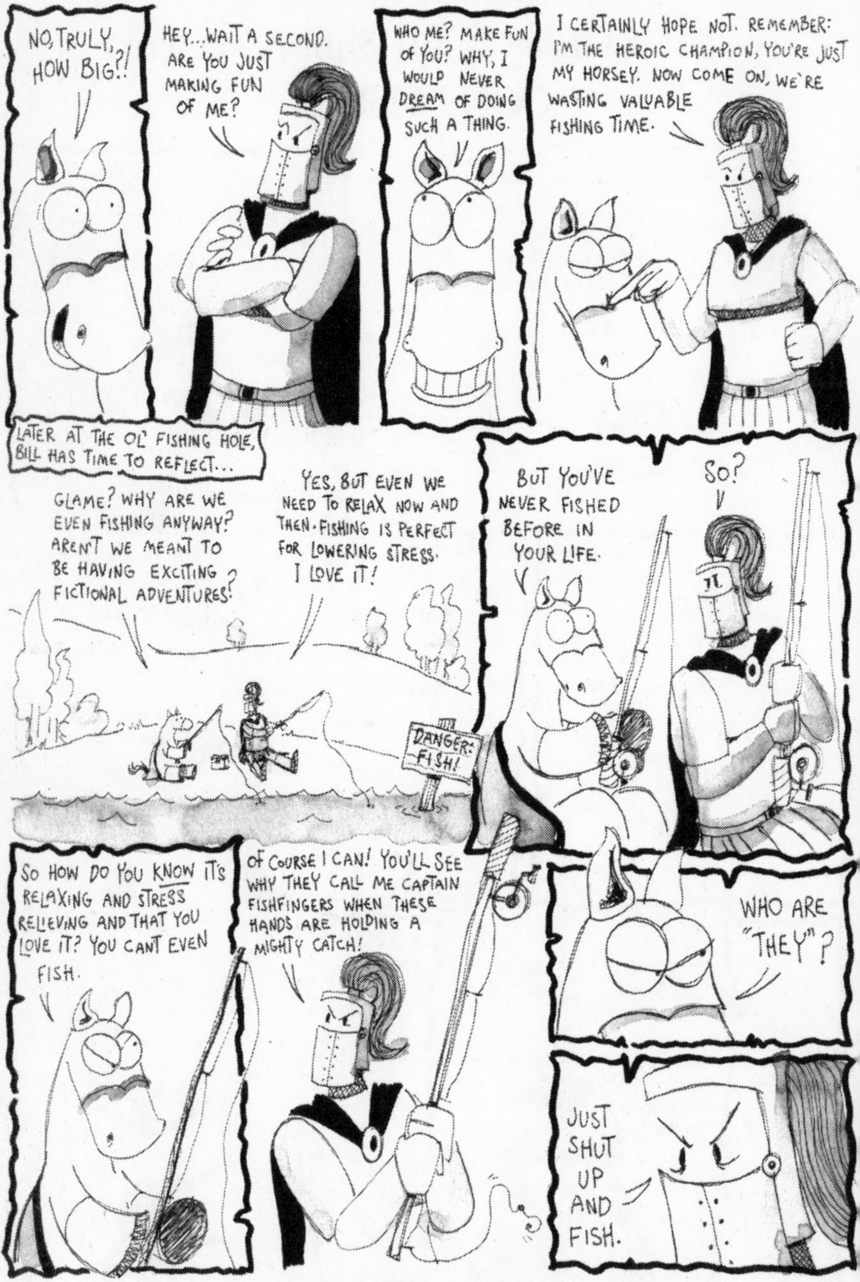
NO, TRULY, HOW BIG?!
HEY... WAIT A SECOND. ARE YOU JUST MAKING FUN OF ME?
WHO ME? MAKE FUN OF YOU? WHY, I WOULD NEVER DREAM OF DOING SUCH A THING.
I CERTAINLY HOPE NOT. REMEMBER: I'M THE HEROIC CHAMPION, YOU'RE JUST MY HORSEY. NOW COME ON, WE'RE WASTING VALUABLE FISHING TIME.
LATER AT THE OL' FISHING HOLE, BILL HAS TIME TO REFLECT...
GLAME? WHY ARE WE EVEN FISHING ANYWAY? AREN'T WE MEANT TO BE HAVING EXCITING FICTIONAL ADVENTURES?
YES, BUT EVEN WE NEED TO RELAX NOW AND THEN. FISHING IS PERFECT FOR LOWERING STRESS. I LOVE IT!
DANGER: FISH!
BUT YOU'VE NEVER FISHED BEFORE IN YOUR LIFE.
SO?
SO HOW DO YOU KNOW IT'S RELAXING AND STRESS RELIEVING AND THAT YOU LOVE IT? YOU CANT EVEN FISH.
OF COURSE I CAN! YOU'LL SEE WHY THEY CALL ME CAPTAIN FISHFINGERS WHEN THESE HANDS ARE HOLDING A MIGHTY CATCH!
WHO ARE "THEY"?
JUST SHUT UP AND FISH.

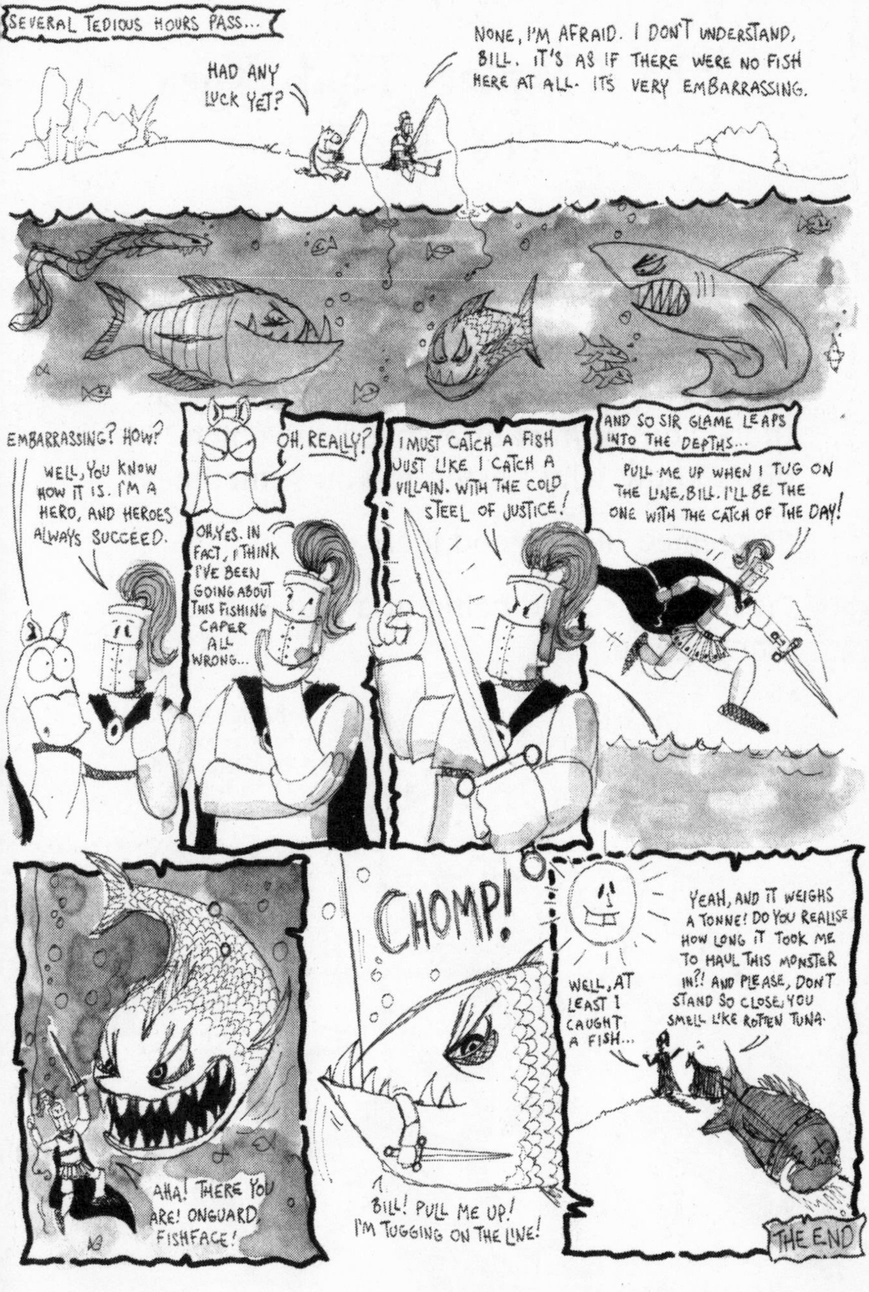
SEVERAL TEDIOUS HOURS PASS...
HAD ANY LUCK YET?
NONE, I'M AFRAID. I DON'T UNDERSTAND, BILL. IT'S AS IF THERE WERE NO FISH HERE AT ALL. IT'S VERY EMBARRASSING.
EMBARRASSING? HOW?
WELL, YOU KNOW HOW IT IS. I'M A HERO, AND HEROES ALWAYS SUCCEED.
OH, REALLY?
OH, YES. IN FACT, I THINK I'VE BEEN GOING ABOUT THIS FISHING CAPER ALL WRONG...
I MUST CATCH A FISH JUST LIKE I CATCH A VILLAIN. WITH THE COLD STEEL OF JUSTICE!
AND SO SIR GLAME LEAPS INTO THE DEPTHS...
PULL ME UP WHEN I TUG ON THE LINE, BILL. I'LL BE THE ONE WITH THE CATCH OF THE DAY!
AHA! THERE YOU ARE! ONGUARD, FISHFACE!
CHOMP!
BILL! PULL ME UP! I'M TUGGING ON THE LINE!
WELL, AT LEAST I CAUGHT A FISH...
YEAH, AND IT WEIGHS A TONNE! DO YOU REALISE HOW LONG IT TOOK ME TO HAUL THIS MONSTER IN?! AND PLEASE, DONT STAND SO CLOSE. YOU SMELL LIKE ROTTEN TUNA.
THE END

The Chapter That Knew Too Much

Sir Glame peeled his flattened head off the ground.

Bill groaned. 'You're a dimwit. What was that? "Run *in front* of a speeding vehicle?" I don't know why I listen to you sometimes.'

'It seemed like a good idea.'

'Yes? Well, so did being in a stupid book starring *you*.'

I BELIEVE THE WORD I AM LOOKING FOR IS "OUCH."

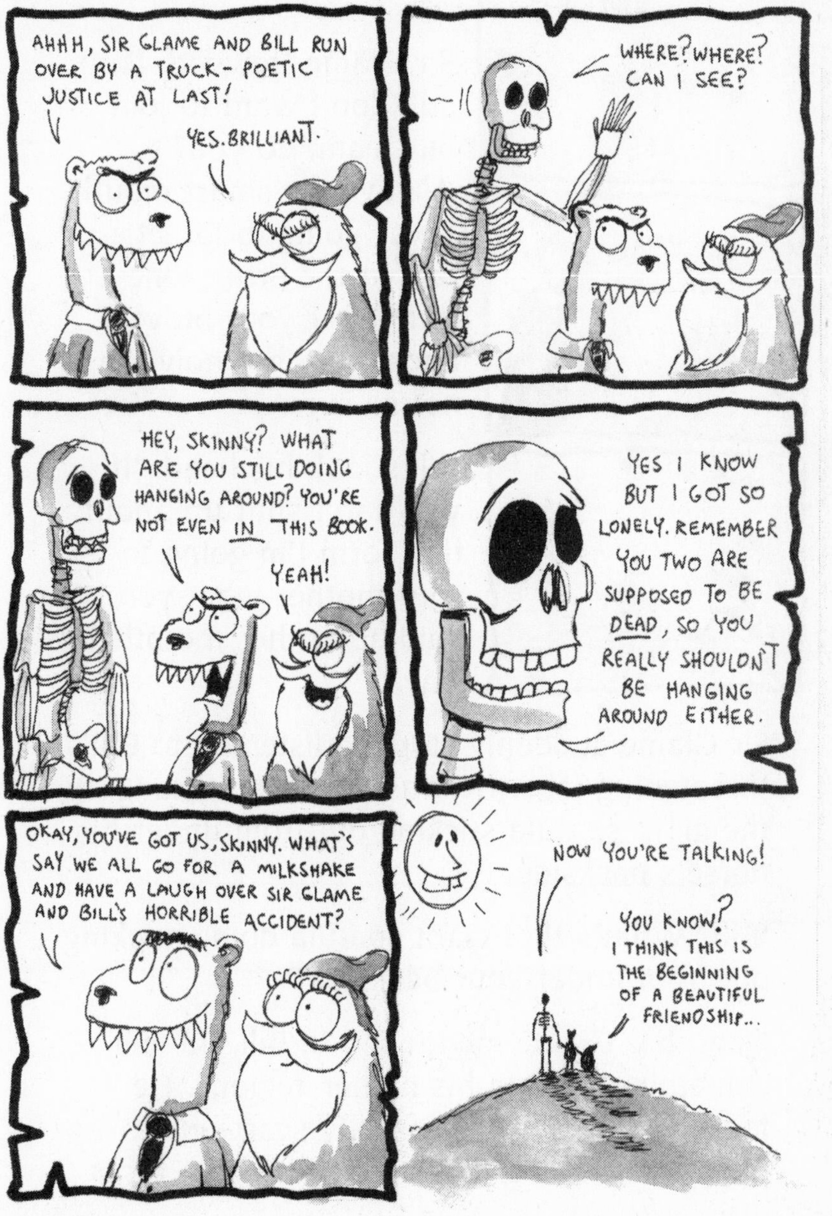
AHHH, SIR GLAME AND BILL RUN OVER BY A TRUCK - POETIC JUSTICE AT LAST!
YES. BRILLIANT.
WHERE? WHERE? CAN I SEE?
HEY, SKINNY? WHAT ARE YOU STILL DOING HANGING AROUND? YOU'RE NOT EVEN IN THIS BOOK.
YEAH!
YES I KNOW BUT I GOT SO LONELY. REMEMBER YOU TWO ARE SUPPOSED TO BE DEAD, SO YOU REALLY SHOULDN'T BE HANGING AROUND EITHER.
OKAY, YOU'VE GOT US, SKINNY. WHAT'S SAY WE ALL GO FOR A MILKSHAKE AND HAVE A LAUGH OVER SIR GLAME AND BILL'S HORRIBLE ACCIDENT?
NOW YOU'RE TALKING!
YOU KNOW? I THINK THIS IS THE BEGINNING OF A BEAUTIFUL FRIENDSHIP...

Sir Glame frowned. 'You still don't want to join our team, do you? Always the smart mouth. I was going to forget about the Strike One form after your bravery back there but now I'm not so sure.'

Bill shook his head. 'If you don't shut up about that form I'm going to tell your mother what you said about her the other day.'

Sir Glame suddenly stopped listening to Bill's threatening jabs. He was too busy looking at the giant spatula sticking out from under his horse's backside.

'Bill? What's that giant spatula doing sticking out from under your backside?'

Now that Glame mentioned it, Bill did feel something tickling his nether-regions. He looked up to see a colossally scary, giant monster scraping him up off the road. If his body hadn't been a twisted, bloody ruin, he would have jumped in fright.

'You great green weed!' cried Sir Glame. 'What are you doing to my faithful steed?'

'Hey, that rhymes!' said Bill. 'Maybe *you* are the mysterious McRascal? Now that *would* be quite a twist. It could almost redeem my faith in this entire adventure.'

Glame shook his head. 'No time for pointless dialogue now, Bill. I think that monster has plans for us!'

The giant beast scraped them up and tossed them in his sack.

COLOSSALLY SCARY MONSTER

'Of course I have plans for you!' the monster roared. 'This is my roadkill spatula. I use it to scrape up the dead animals that get splattered along this highway. I put them in my roadkill sack.'

HIYA KIDS!

'This isn't a highway,' said Bill from inside the sack. 'There are no highways in fantasy stories.'

'Shut up in there!' The monster punched the sack. 'You two may not technically be dead, but that doesn't mean you're not up for pickings. Now I'm gunna take you back to my lair where my evil will continue, except in a gloomier setting.'

The giant monster threw the sack over his shoulder and set off home to his lair.

'What do you think he's going to do to us?' Sir Glame asked Bill. 'Try and eat us maybe?'

'No, no. That would be too obvious. It's bound to be something ridiculous and contrived. We'll have to have a boxing match with his pet goldfish or help him paint his living room or something stupid like that.'

Soon enough the monster arrived back at his cave in the mountains. He threw the sack onto the ground and Bill and Sir Glame tumbled out.

'Owww!' Bill groaned. 'Take it easy! I think I've punctured my intestines!'

'Indeed,' said Sir Glame. 'Those wheels went right over my pelvis.'

'Stop your whinging!' growled the monster.

MONSTER'S
(COSY) MOUNTAIN
LAIR

Suddenly from the lair's shadows, another beast appeared. It looked just like the first, except it had longer eyelashes and wore a bow on its head.

'Yes, you two shut your holes!' the new monster said. 'We've got work to do.'

Sir Glame and Bill wondered what villainy they had planned. Luckily, the monsters had a sudden urge to explain exactly what they were up to.

'Let me introduce myself,' the first monster said. 'My name is Mongo, and this is my sister, Bongo. I am a Hydra and so is she – '

'Wait on,' Glame butted in, 'perhaps you'd better explain what a Hydra is for the good of our young readers.'

'I will not!' said Mongo. 'That's what the pictures are for. I can't help it if your dopey readers aren't up on their Greek Mythology.'

NO
JUNK MAIL

'Hey, aren't Hydras meant to have multiple heads?' asked Bill. 'You two have only got one each.'

'Stop interrupting me!' glared Mongo. 'I'm getting to that. Me and my sister are Hydras who were unfortunately born deformed. We each only have one head.'

'Yes,' Bongo sighed. 'It's been so stigmatising for us.'

Bill frowned. 'Don't try to impress us with big words like "stigmatising". I enjoy teasing people different to myself, you know. Especially freaks like you two.'

Sir Glame nodded. 'I once had a cousin who was deformed. His name was Dale. He was so bad, my aunt had to carry him around in a bucket. Everyone called him Dale in the Pail.'

THE ONLY PROBLEM YOU'LL FACE WITH HAVING A HUGE PILE OF ROTTING ANIMALS IN YOUR HOUSE WILL BE RESISTING THE URGE TO EAT THEM.

'Well, Me and Bongo won't be deformed for much longer. We use the roadkill I gather to practise a little operation we're working on.' The one-headed Hydra pulled back a nearby curtain. Behind him was an operating table and a rack of surgical tools. Next to the table was a disgusting pile of dead animals bizarrely stitched together. There was a half-rabbit half-squirrel, a half-seagull half-chimpanzee and a half-turkey half-mackerel, just to name a few.

'Good Gravy! What ghastly work is this? You *sew* two creatures together to try and make them one?'

'Not ghastly, knight,' said Bongo, 'we're just trying to get it right so we can finally do the operation on ourselves. Then we can have two heads on the same body and be a normal Hydra just as nature intended.'

Mongo slipped into his surgical gown. 'Get the knock-out gas ready, sister.' He lumbered towards our heroes. 'Now hold still, you two, this won't hurt a bit.'

'Wait, wait!' Bill insisted. 'Perhaps before you preform your hideous procedure on us, I could favour you with an amusing limerick from this book?' and he whipped out **Saucy McRascal's Big Book of Fun**.

'Good thinking, Bill,' Sir Glame whispered. 'They'll be so disgusted by that deviant's twisted verses we'll be able to make our escape!'

Mongo and Bongo agreed. 'Okay then, horse-like creature. Tell us one of your poems.'

'I think you'll really be able to relate to this one,' said Bill. 'It's called *Let's Play Doctor*...

> *'Teddy just had a heart attack,*
> *dolly's guts are on the floor.*
> *Humpty broke his head apart,*
> *and his shattered legs are sore.*
> *Bunny has thrown up his guts,*
> *the place is green with sick.*
> *Telephone the doctor,*
> *I hope he will be quick.'*

Mongo cheered. 'Ahh, what a happy, happy

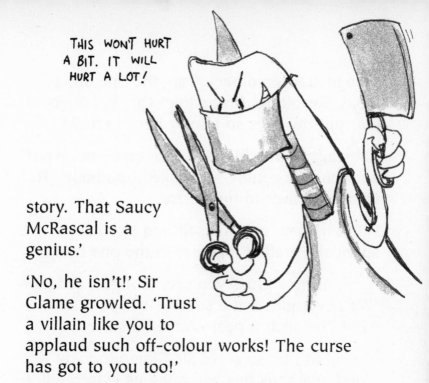

THIS WON'T HURT
A BIT. IT WILL
HURT A LOT!

story. That Saucy
McRascal is a
genius.'

'No, he isn't!' Sir
Glame growled. 'Trust
a villain like you to
applaud such off-colour works! The curse
has got to you too!'

'Enough!' Mongo declared. 'Gas this yokel.
He has no appreciation of fine literature!'

Sir Glame and Bill tried to struggle, but their
pretzel-shaped bodies were no use. Bongo
came over to them with the knock-out gas...

*   *   *

'The horror!' Bongo gasped. 'The
unspeakable horror!'

Sir Glame opened his eyes as the gas wore
off. 'What? What is it?'

Mongo staggered back from the operating table. 'Revolting! Disgusting! Quick, Bongo, tear out my eyes so I don't have to look!'

Bill staggered to his feet. 'Oh, come on, what are you two getting so honked up about?' He wandered over to the mirror.

What he saw was himself and Sir Glame, surgically grafted together in the one body.

'Look at how gross you are!' Bongo cried. 'We never guessed a successful operation would be such a pear-shaped disaster!'

'I wouldn't be so sure,' Sir Glame thought aloud. 'Perhaps this will bring us closer, Bill. I think some quality time is just what we need.'

Bill took a long hard look in the mirror and groaned. 'Even I wasn't expecting something as ridiculous as this. I refuse to participate in the rest of this chapter.'

Glame looked at Bill.
Mongo looked at Glame
and Bill. Bongo looked at Mongo
and Glame and Bill. Glame looked at
Mongo and Bongo. Everyone shrugged. Bill
said nothing.

'Oh well,' Sir Glame sighed. 'I guess we're
done then. See you guys later.'

The two Hydras waved them goodbye.

This chapter
ends here.

A Sir Glame & Bill Mini-Adventure
THE VILLAIN IN THE MIRROR

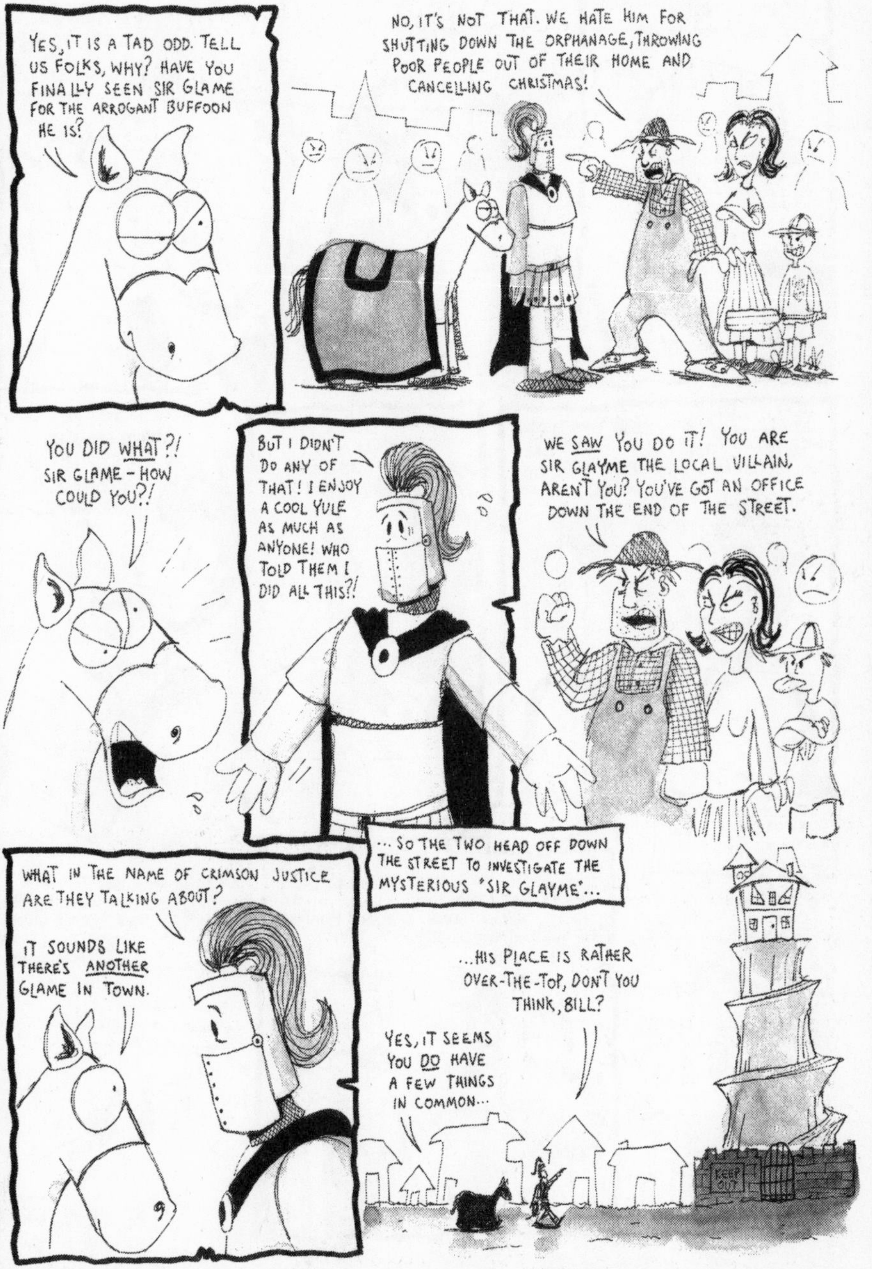
YES, IT IS A TAD ODD. TELL US FOLKS, WHY? HAVE YOU FINALLY SEEN SIR GLAME FOR THE ARROGANT BUFFOON HE IS?
NO, IT'S NOT THAT. WE HATE HIM FOR SHUTTING DOWN THE ORPHANAGE, THROWING POOR PEOPLE OUT OF THEIR HOME AND CANCELLING CHRISTMAS!
YOU DID WHAT?! SIR GLAME - HOW COULD YOU?!
BUT I DIDN'T DO ANY OF THAT! I ENJOY A COOL YULE AS MUCH AS ANYONE! WHO TOLD THEM I DID ALL THIS?!
WE SAW YOU DO IT! YOU ARE SIR GLAYME THE LOCAL VILLAIN, AREN'T YOU? YOU'VE GOT AN OFFICE DOWN THE END OF THE STREET.
WHAT IN THE NAME OF CRIMSON JUSTICE ARE THEY TALKING ABOUT?
IT SOUNDS LIKE THERE'S ANOTHER GLAME IN TOWN.
... SO THE TWO HEAD OFF DOWN THE STREET TO INVESTIGATE THE MYSTERIOUS 'SIR GLAYME'...
...HIS PLACE IS RATHER OVER-THE-TOP, DON'T YOU THINK, BILL?
YES, IT SEEMS YOU DO HAVE A FEW THINGS IN COMMON...
KEEP OUT

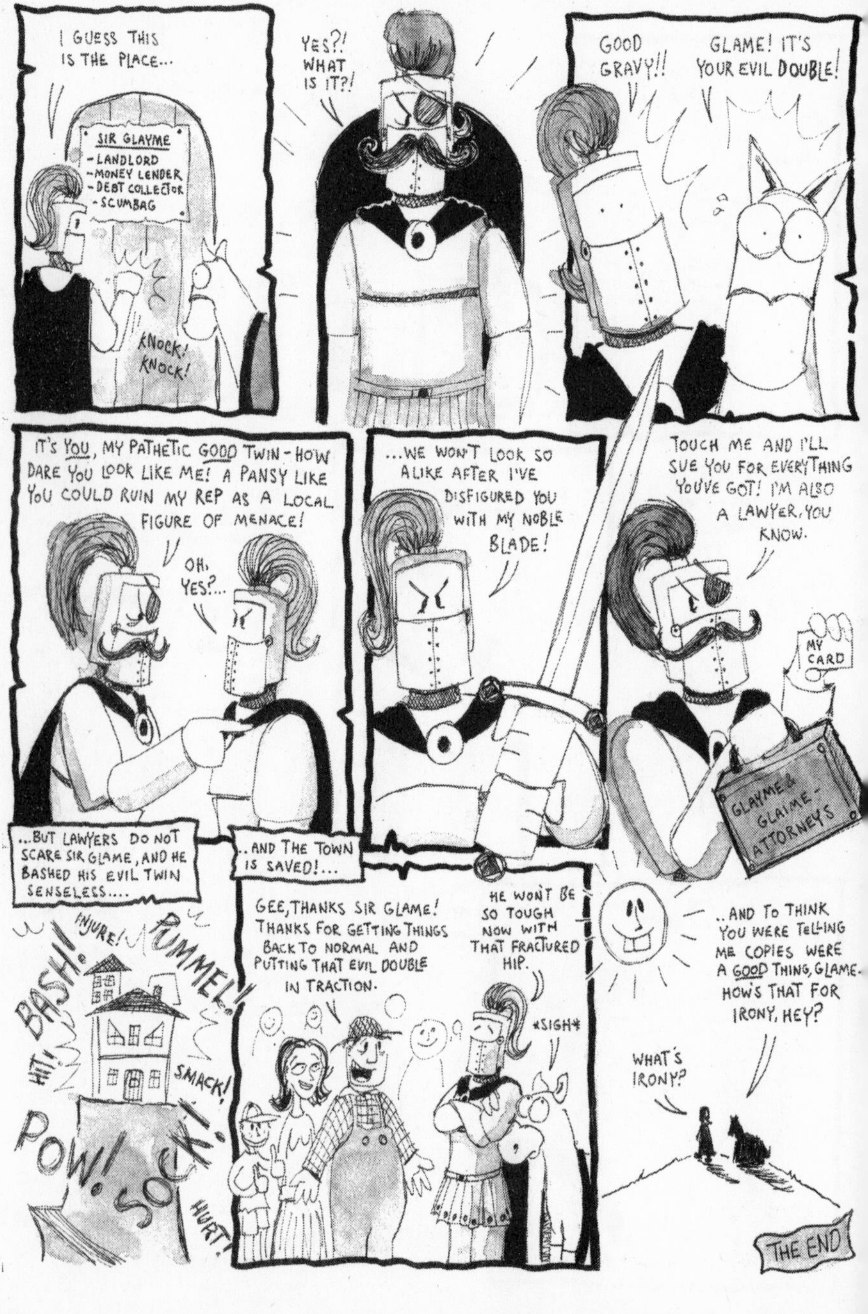
I GUESS THIS IS THE PLACE...
SIR GLAYME
- LANDLORD
- MONEY LENDER
- DEBT COLLECTOR
- SCUMBAG
KNOCK! KNOCK!
YES?! WHAT IS IT?!
GOOD GRAVY!!
GLAME! IT'S YOUR EVIL DOUBLE!
IT'S YOU, MY PATHETIC GOOD TWIN - HOW DARE YOU LOOK LIKE ME! A PANSY LIKE YOU COULD RUIN MY REP AS A LOCAL FIGURE OF MENACE!
OH, YES?...
...WE WON'T LOOK SO ALIKE AFTER I'VE DISFIGURED YOU WITH MY NOBLE BLADE!
TOUCH ME AND I'LL SUE YOU FOR EVERYTHING YOU'VE GOT! I'M ALSO A LAWYER, YOU KNOW.
MY CARD
GLAYME & GLAIME - ATTORNEYS
...BUT LAWYERS DO NOT SCARE SIR GLAME, AND HE BASHED HIS EVIL TWIN SENSELESS....
INJURE!
PUMMEL!
BASH!
HIT!
SMACK!
POW!
SOCK!
HURT!
..AND THE TOWN IS SAVED!...
GEE, THANKS SIR GLAME! THANKS FOR GETTING THINGS BACK TO NORMAL AND PUTTING THAT EVIL DOUBLE IN TRACTION.
HE WON'T BE SO TOUGH NOW WITH THAT FRACTURED HIP.
SIGH
..AND TO THINK YOU WERE TELLING ME COPIES WERE A GOOD THING, GLAME. HOW'S THAT FOR IRONY, HEY?
WHAT'S IRONY?
THE END

The Chapter That Failed Grade One

Sir Glame and Bill walked back down the mountain together. In fact, they were very together since they were sharing the same body. If you saw them in the street you'd run screaming at their freakiness, or point your finger and make fun of them.

'Of course we look freaky,' said Bill to that last paragraph. 'All we're good for now is hiding at the bottom of some black lagoon and scaring slack-jawed tourists.'

'I think you're being unfair, Bill. Our good half reckons this could work for the best.'

Bill turned to face his other head, Sir Glame. 'The good half being you, I suppose? Trust me, there is no way this could work out to our advantage. We're a mutant and our quest is just one poorly-linked, no-direction happening after the next.'

'Not so,' said Glame. 'Our quest is going fine. See that sign over there?'

'*Another* sign?' Bill looked. 'Where?'

'It says *Village of Jiggy – 1 mile*. And notice the writing on the sign? It's the same black writing as on the King's note. I'd say that's a very big clue.'

Bill squinted. There was nothing around but the mountain where they'd just left the Hydras. 'I still don't see any sign. I think you're making it up.'

Sir Glame started walking. 'I'll prove it. We're going to Jiggy and I bet we'll find Saucy McRascal there.' The knight also took out a Strike Two form and began filling it out.

'Hey, what are you doing?'

'I'm sick of your attitude, Bill. All you do is make smart remarks. You've forced me to do this. When the King sees this Strike Two form, he'll know that you're not performing. It really is a shame. You'd better pull up your socks, Mister.'

Bill frowned. 'I'm not sure what insults me more: your stupid form, or that you're using my arm to help you fill it out. Stick to your own side of the body.'

'But I'm right-handed,' Glame moaned.

'Tough luck,' and Bill refused to let his hand help in filling out the Strike Two.

By the time they reached Jiggy, Glame had managed to complete the form himself.

Jiggy was a typical village you might find in a fantasy setting. Medieval looking houses, muddy streets and really not much else.

Sir Glame and Bill looked around. The little town seemed deserted.

'All I see is muddy streets and medieval buildings,' Glame said. 'Really not much else.'

'Where is everyone?' Bill wondered.

'Look.' Glame pointed to dozens of footprints in the mud. They led to the town hall at the end of the main street. Our two heroes followed the prints to the front door.

WE MUST REMEMBER TO WIPE OUR FEET BEFORE WE GO IN, BILL..

JIGGY MUNICIPAL CENTRE

It sounded like there was some sort of
meeting going on inside.

'What do you think?' said Sir Glame.

'About what?' said Bill.

'About the door.'

'What about it?'

'Do you think we should go in?'

'I will if you will.'

'Okay then...'

'Okay then what?'

'Okay. We'll go in.'

'Well, go on.'

'Go on what?'

'Turn the handle.'

'Oh.' Glame blushed. 'Sorry.'

The hall was filled with every villager in the district. Up on stage were twenty girls, all wearing swimsuits. A man in a fancy suit stood amongst them. In one corner a brass band played a jolly tune. Above the stage a banner read: *The 121st Annual Miss Jiggy Beauty Pageant.*

The hall door slammed behind them.

Bill groaned. 'Oh no.'

The pageant stopped. The host paused. Everyone turned to look.

'Don't mind us,' said Glame, 'I just need to ask you all a few questions.'

The man in the suit looked down at the half-knight half-horse mutant.

'If you don't mind, we *are* in the middle of something here,' the host said. Villagers mumbled their agreement. 'Unless you're a spectator or a contestant, you'll have to leave.'

The knight suddenly had an idea.

Bill turned to Sir Glame. 'No way. Don't even *think* about it.'

Glame grinned. 'So you think we're ugly, do you? Well, I'll prove you wrong.'

*   *   *

Sir Glame and Bill stood on stage wearing a bikini. Beside them were the most glamorous gals Jiggy had to offer.

'Well, folks,' the host declared, 'isn't our newest entry the most...um...unique little lady you've ever laid eyes on. Now, dear, why don't you tell us a bit about yourself?'

'My name is Sir Glame and this is my horse, Bill. We both share the same body since two mutant Hydras kidnapped us and performed a hideously disfiguring operation. Other than that, I like long walks in the rain and candlelit dinners, and my life partner here enjoys eating sugar cubes.'

'That's wonderful,' said the host.

'I enjoy candlelit dinners too,' said Bill.

'Yes, don't we all,' the host said to the crowd. 'Well, you both sound like very deep characters. However, every girl who enters the Jiggy pageant has to perform a little talent act for us. Something to prove they're not just a pretty face. Since you came in last, you're the only ones who haven't performed yet. What have you got for us?'

'Remind me again why we're doing this?' hissed Bill.

'No time for explanations,' Glame whispered back. 'We have to think of a talent fast. Luckily, it's a well-known fact that the prettier you are, the less personality you have. By the look of these bimbos, they must have only one brain between them. We're sure to win.'

'Well, who's a bitter boy then?' Bill grinned. 'I always wondered why you never take off your helmet. Don't worry your ugly little head, Glame. I've got an idea.'

'It's not another Saucy McRascal poem, is it?' Glame frowned.

'No, no. It's something much more tasteful. You just watch and see.'

The host and the crowd still waited.

'Ladies and gentlemen!' Bill addressed the hall. 'Prepare to be blown away! *Here* is *our* talent!'

He pulled Sir Glame's sword out of its scabbard and with one quick chop, cut his arm clean off.

EEK!

CHOP!!

'Hey, that's my arm!' Glame frowned. 'I needed that!'

The crowd gaped with awe.

'Wow!' the host declared. 'Self-masochism! That's quite a talent!'

'You should see my whole act. I commit suicide as a finale.'

Everyone cheered at Glame's bloody arm

lying on the stage. The other contestants kicked themselves for not being as gifted as Bill. The judges quickly deliberated. Soon the host was handed a card.

'Attention everyone,' he called. 'By unanimous vote, Sir Glame and Bill are this year's Miss Jiggy Beauty Queen!'

Sir Glame and Bill were showered in flowers and given a sash to wear. They ponced around on stage showing off to the crowd. Sir Glame was especially proud.

'See Bill, I told you my plan would work.'

'But how does winning a beauty pageant lead us to the mysterious McRascal?'

'Umm,' Glame scratched his head. 'Let me get back to you on that.'

'Don't worry about it.' The horse wiped a happy tear from his eye and waved to the admiring villagers. 'I've never felt more beautiful.'

A Sir Glame & Bill Mini-Adventure
GLAME REACHES OUT

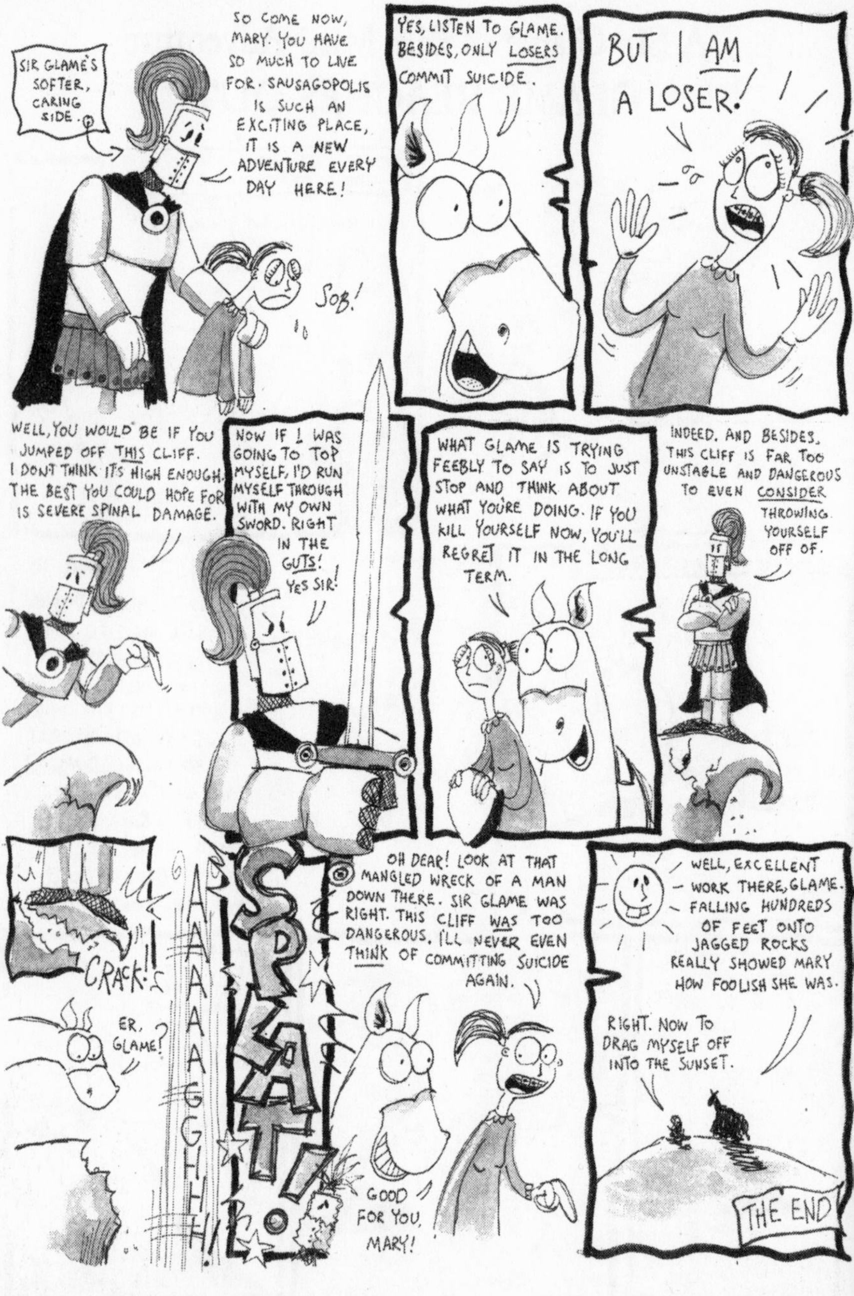
SIR GLAME'S SOFTER, CARING SIDE.
SO COME NOW, MARY. YOU HAVE SO MUCH TO LIVE FOR. SAUSAGOPOLIS IS SUCH AN EXCITING PLACE, IT IS A NEW ADVENTURE EVERY DAY HERE!
SOB!
YES, LISTEN TO GLAME. BESIDES, ONLY LOSERS COMMIT SUICIDE.
BUT I AM A LOSER!
WELL, YOU WOULD BE IF YOU JUMPED OFF THIS CLIFF. I DON'T THINK IT'S HIGH ENOUGH. THE BEST YOU COULD HOPE FOR IS SEVERE SPINAL DAMAGE.
NOW IF I WAS GOING TO TOP MYSELF, I'D RUN MYSELF THROUGH WITH MY OWN SWORD. RIGHT IN THE GUTS! YES SIR!
WHAT GLAME IS TRYING FEEBLY TO SAY IS TO JUST STOP AND THINK ABOUT WHAT YOU'RE DOING. IF YOU KILL YOURSELF NOW, YOU'LL REGRET IT IN THE LONG TERM.
INDEED. AND BESIDES, THIS CLIFF IS FAR TOO UNSTABLE AND DANGEROUS TO EVEN CONSIDER THROWING YOURSELF OFF OF.
CRACK!
ER, GLAME?
AAAAAAAGGHH!
SPLAT!
OH DEAR! LOOK AT THAT MANGLED WRECK OF A MAN DOWN THERE. SIR GLAME WAS RIGHT. THIS CLIFF WAS TOO DANGEROUS. I'LL NEVER EVEN THINK OF COMMITTING SUICIDE AGAIN.
GOOD FOR YOU, MARY!
WELL, EXCELLENT WORK THERE, GLAME. FALLING HUNDREDS OF FEET ONTO JAGGED ROCKS REALLY SHOWED MARY HOW FOOLISH SHE WAS.
RIGHT. NOW TO DRAG MYSELF OFF INTO THE SUNSET.
THE END

The Chapter With No Name

After many hugs and kisses from the adoring villagers, our two mutant heroes decided to return to their quest. They left Jiggy in search of Saucy McRascal once more.

They journeyed across the grassy plains of Sausagopolis until they came to the base of a majestic mountain range.

Bill looked up to the mountain's peak. 'Wow. It's almost slopping over with majestic-ness, hey, Glame?'

I'D CALL MYSELF MORE SCENIC THAN MAJESTIC.

They are the Great Mountains, Bill. I have a feeling the answers we're looking for are up there. You know the legend about them, don't you?'

REALLY? I CALL MYSELF KEVIN.

'I do, but tell me again for the good of our young readers.'

Glame nodded. 'Legend has it that the God of Thunder, Dooboo-Crackerwhack, lives on a storm cloud above the

DooBOO
CRACKER
WHACK
→

I'VE GOT A CURE FOR THOSE
TWO MORTAL EGO MANIACS.
A FEW MILLION VOLTS OUGHT
TO FIX THEM UP PERMANENTLY.

SMITING
BOLTS

highest peak. He controls
the weather in
Sausagopolis. For our
sakes, I hope he's in
a calm mood
today.'

'If he *is* up there, I
want a word with him.
I'm fed up with all this
rain we've been getting. I hate
having to put my horse blanket in the dryer.
Plus those carrots I planted last month got
completely washed out.'

The clouds above the Great Mountains began
to rumble.

'Steady Bill,' said Glame. 'You don't want to
offend the Gods.'

'Oh, but I do. Who does Dooboo-
Crackerwhack think
he's fooling
anyway?

I'M REALLY
LOOKING FORWARD
TO THE "I HATE
SIR GLAME AND
BILL" PARTY.
I EVEN BOUGHT
MYSELF A
NEW BOW!

I MAY
EVEN GET
MY HAIR
CUT.

He can't control the weather. It's controlled by the atmosphere, with respect to variables such as temperature, moisture, wind velocity, and barometric pressure. It's not run by just some mouldy old beardo wearing a bed sheet and throwing thunderbolts about.'

Suddenly out of a clear blue sky, Sir Glame and Bill were struck by lightning!

'Good Gravy!' Sir Glame lay flat on his back. 'Where did that come from?'

'How about that for luck?' Bill got back up. 'The jolt of electricity blew us apart again. I thought we'd be stuck together forever.'

Sir Glame examined himself. 'You're right, Bill. Look, I've even got my arm back. I'll bet it was a gift from Dooboo-Crackerwhack. He wanted to prove his power to your doubting eyes.'

'More like he was trying to kill us with one of his nasty jolts,' Bill scoffed. 'What a klutz. If he can't even finish us off, what chance has he possibly got controlling the weather?'

Sir Glame suggested they get moving before the Thunder God took another crack at them.

They pressed on up the mountain path. It wasn't long before they came to a crossroad, just as the climb became steep. A signpost in the middle read:

RIGHT = DEATH.

LEFT = A FATE WORSE THAN DEATH.

Beside the post stood a hunchbacked woman.

'*More* signs?' groaned Bill.

'What does this sign mean, old woman?' Sir Glame asked her. 'Death or a fate worse than death? Is there something we should know?'

'Nothing I don't know already, sonny,' the hunchback said smugly.

PSST! DO YOU WANT TO KNOW BILL'S LOGIN PASSWORD? IT'S "STALLION". HA HA HA!

'Who are you anyway?' Bill frowned. 'You look like a witch. You've cast some lousy spell up there, haven't you?'

'Me, a witch? Dear me, no. Magic is yesterday's news. I work with computers. Allow me to introduce myself.' The woman gave Sir Glame her business card. It read: *KAREN WANGIDDY WANG WANG – LOCAL KNOW-IT-ALL.* 'If you want me to tell you what the sign means, it will cost you. I don't work for free.'

'Who ever heard of a witch called Karen?' Bill shook his head.

'I told you: I'm *not* a witch. I'm a computer consultant.'

Sir Glame frowned. 'You've got no business being into computers in Sausagopolis. This is a fantasy setting. There's supposed to be no such thing as computers here.'

'You're like a lot of people I talk to, pretending they don't need to know,' Karen scoffed. 'Information technology is the future. My business is booming because of dummies like you.'

'How much do you charge for advice then?' ask Bill.

'Fifty dollars an hour. Sixty on weekends.'

'That's outrageous,' said Glame.

'I'm afraid that's the going rate,' Karen yawned. 'You're not going to find anyone around here who knows more than me.

You'd better ask me now before I take a better offer from someone else.'

I'M READY TO GET X-TREME!

'Who else?' Bill looked around. 'We're the only ones here!'

Karen rolled her eyes. 'You just don't understand the way the world works, hey Sonny?'

Sir Glame gave up. 'Come on, Bill. Let's go. This woman is clearly insane.'

So the two heroes turned right and kept clambering up the mountain.

'You'll be back!' Karen called.

After another hour of climbing, Glame and Bill reached the top. They found themselves standing before a huge, crumbling castle. It looked just like one of those spooky old ones ghosts love. Storm clouds gathered around it and bats flew in and out the windows.

'You suppose Count Dracula is in there?' said Bill. 'Or maybe Saucy McRascal?'

PRETTY CREEPY,
AIN'T I?

'I don't know.' Glame drew his
sword. 'But we're going
to find out.'

The two heroes walked up to the
castle gate. The drawbridge was
raised and there was no way
across. A cavernous drop went
down, down, down the edge of
the cliff. Sir Glame thought about
jumping, but with all his armour
on he knew he'd fall like a barrel
full of bronzed monkeys.

Now what were they
going to do?

Bill noticed there was a tiny
spider sitting on a rock
nearby. It was smoking a pipe
and smiling contentedly to
itself.

'Do you know who lives
here?' Bill asked it.

'My name is Max,'
said the spider.

THIS WAY
FOR EVIL

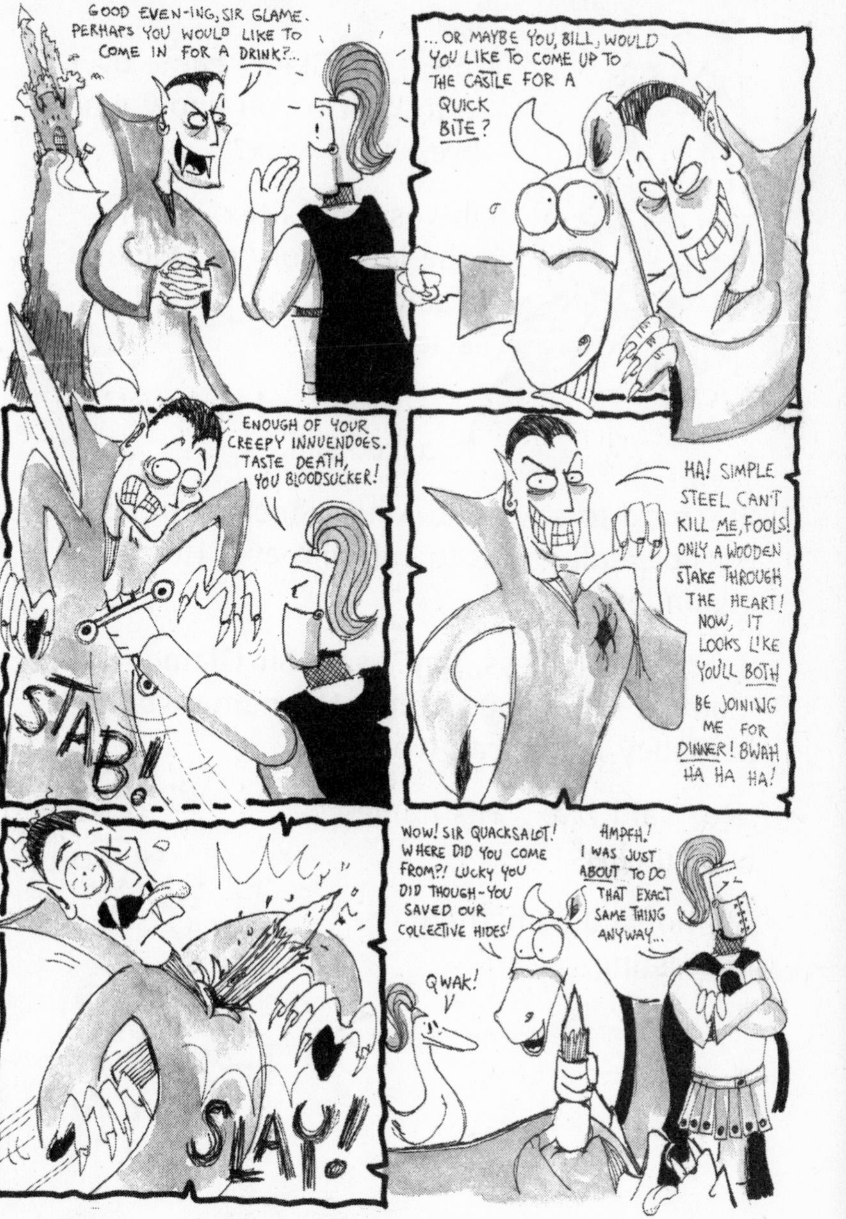
GOOD EVEN-ING, SIR GLAME. PERHAPS YOU WOULD LIKE TO COME IN FOR A DRINK?..
...OR MAYBE YOU, BILL, WOULD YOU LIKE TO COME UP TO THE CASTLE FOR A QUICK BITE?
ENOUGH OF YOUR CREEPY INNUENDOES. TASTE DEATH, YOU BLOODSUCKER!
STAB!!
HA! SIMPLE STEEL CAN'T KILL ME, FOOLS! ONLY A WOODEN STAKE THROUGH THE HEART! NOW, IT LOOKS LIKE YOU'LL BOTH BE JOINING ME FOR DINNER! BWAH HA HA HA!
SLAY!!
WOW! SIR QUACKSALOT! WHERE DID YOU COME FROM?! LUCKY YOU DID THOUGH-YOU SAVED OUR COLLECTIVE HIDES!
HMPFH! I WAS JUST ABOUT TO DO THAT EXACT SAME THING ANYWAY...
QWAK!

GIDDAY KIDS PULL UP A ROCK AND JOIN ME.

MAX'S ROCK

Sir Glame came over to it. 'Do you know who lives here, Max?'

'Oh yes,' said Max. 'That is the laboratory of Doctor Nameless. He's a mad scientist.'

'An *evil* mad scientist?' asked Bill.

'It's hard to say,' said Max. 'Since he's mad it's not really right to call him evil. He's just misunderstood.'

'Doctor Nameless, hey?' said Sir Glame. 'Sounds suspicious to me. His name wouldn't be Saucy McRascal, would it?'

'No,' said Max. 'His name is Nameless.'

Bill noticed something interesting.

I KNOW SMOKING IS BAD FOR ME, BUT I'M ONLY IN THIS ONE CHAPTER SO I REALLY DON'T CARE.

The *SAUSAGOPOLIS SCRAP* truck that had run them over a few chapters ago was parked in the castle courtyard.

'Is that Dr Nameless's truck?'

'Certainly,' Max puffed his pipe. 'Dr Nameless's assistant, Goggles the Mutant, drives that truck. The Doctor built a giant robot for that movie shooting in the forest. The man is very good with his hands.'

Sir Glame was pleased the spider was so helpful.

'See Bill?' he beamed. 'Now we're making

progress. The quest isn't directionless after all. I told you this story had a plot.'

Bill ignored him. 'Is there a way we can get into this castle?' he asked.

'Oh yes,' said Max. 'Go back down to the crossroad and turn left at the signpost.'

Bill scratched his head. 'But doesn't that way lead to "a fate worse than death"?'

'It doesn't matter, Bill,' said Sir Glame. 'This is the first real lead we've had. I've got a feeling the answer to Sausagopolis's curse is somewhere in that castle.' He started walking back down to the road.

Bill didn't have any better ideas, so he followed along.

When they arrived back at the crossroads, Karen Wangiddy Wang Wang was waiting.

'See?' she grinned. 'What

did I tell you? You faced certain death that way, didn't you? You just didn't want to listen. You thought you knew it all. And now you've had to come crawling back for my help.'

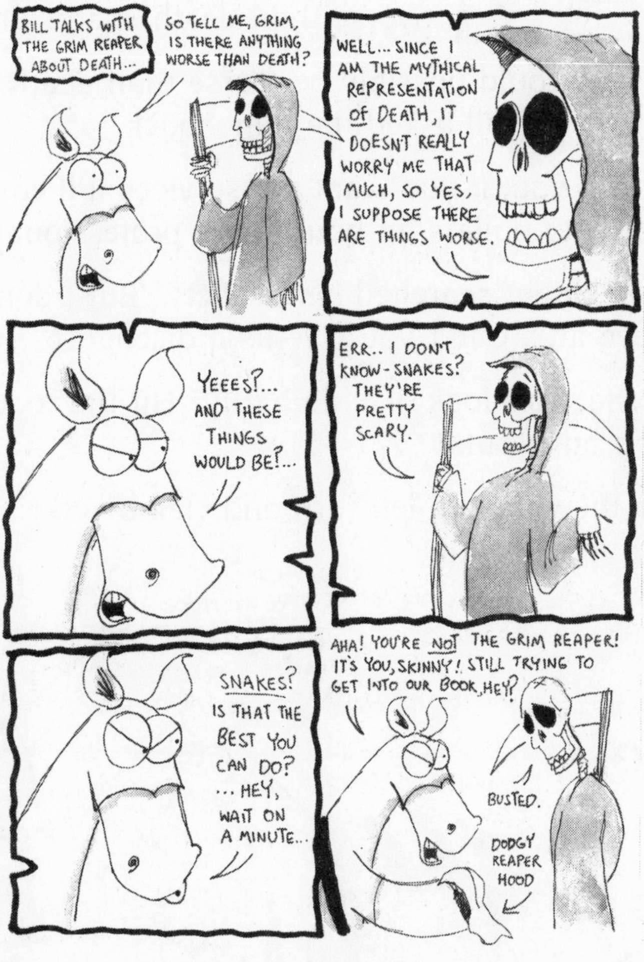
BILL TALKS WITH THE GRIM REAPER ABOUT DEATH...
SO TELL ME, GRIM, IS THERE ANYTHING WORSE THAN DEATH?
WELL... SINCE I AM THE MYTHICAL REPRESENTATION OF DEATH, IT DOESN'T REALLY WORRY ME THAT MUCH, SO YES, I SUPPOSE THERE ARE THINGS WORSE.
YEEES?... AND THESE THINGS WOULD BE?...
ERR.. I DON'T KNOW - SNAKES? THEY'RE PRETTY SCARY.
SNAKES? IS THAT THE BEST YOU CAN DO? ... HEY, WAIT ON A MINUTE...
AHA! YOU'RE NOT THE GRIM REAPER! IT'S YOU, SKINNY! STILL TRYING TO GET INTO OUR BOOK, HEY?
BUSTED.
DODGY REAPER HOOD

'We didn't face any death at all,' said Glame. 'We couldn't even get into the castle. A friendly spider told us we have to go left. Up the "fate worse than death" path.'

'What could possibly be worse than death anyway?' Bill asked the hunchback.

'I told you, if you want my services it'll cost you fifty dollars an hour. I'm a professional.'

The knight searched his pockets. 'But I don't have fifty. Can't you give us a discount?'

'What do I look like: a charity? Hit the road, you burn-outs.'

So they made a left turn and clambered off up the path.

Sir Glame had a nagging urge to go back and choke Karen with her own tongue. When they finally reached the end of the path, they found it led them to exactly the same place – Doctor Nameless's castle.

'I don't understand,' said Sir Glame.

Bill kicked himself. 'I can't believe what idiots we are!'

The castle's drawbridge was still up. Max the spider was still there too. He sat on his rock, but now beside him was another spider. The new spider wore a bright yellow blazer and had a golf bag slung over his shoulder.

Bill growled. 'Hey, Max! You said the left turn would get us inside the castle. It just brought us back here!'

Max giggled. 'Yes, I know.'

The other spider spoke up. 'Hello. My Name is Rex. You'll have to excuse my evil twin brother, Max. He's quite screwy, you know. He loves harassing people and putting them in deadly situations. I think he hoped you'd fall off the mountain.'

'Yes indeed,' Max took a big suck on his

'Yes indeedy,' Max took a big suck on his pipe. 'I'm surprised you didn't. It's quite slippery, that left path. I was looking forward to a big splat!'

'Well, *here's* one for you then.' Sir Glame went over and stepped on Max. – SPLAT! – He calmly scraped the mess off his boot. 'It just so happens I like putting evil twin brothers in deadly situations.'

Rex sighed. 'I told him smoking would kill him one day, but he never listened to me. I wanted him to take up golf like me. It's very invigorating. Plenty of fresh air and exercise.'

'Just tell us how to get into the wretched castle,' said Bill.

The spider moved to one side of his rock.
Next to him was a big red button. It said:
PRESS TO OPEN DRAWBRIDGE.

'I'm sorry,' Rex said. 'I must have been sitting
on that all along.'

Not wanting to waste any more
time, Sir Glame quickly pressed
the button and our two heroes
rushed inside. Ten minutes later
Rex the spider was eaten by
a wandering duck.

A Sir Glame & Bill Mini-Adventure
LITTLE JOHNNY NEEDS A KIDNEY

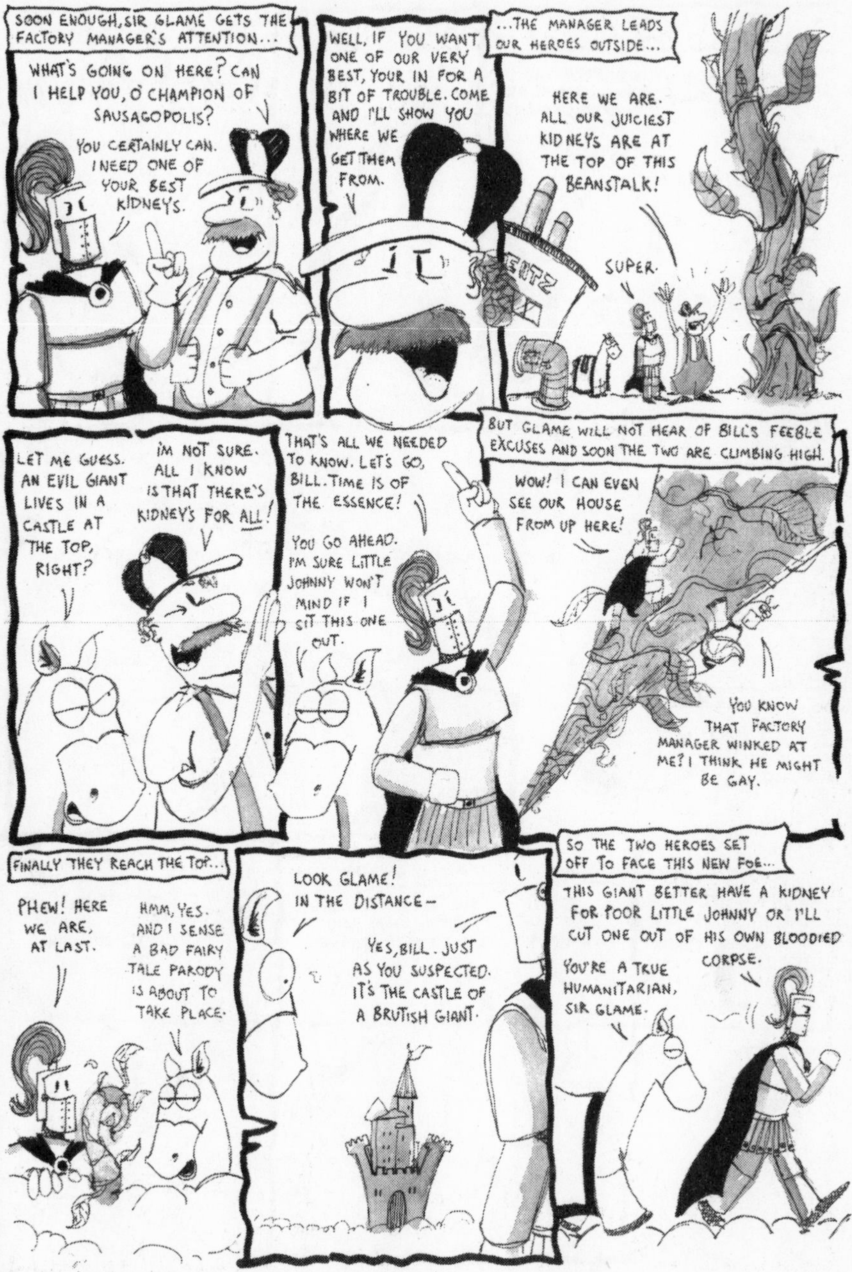
SOON ENOUGH, SIR GLAME GETS THE FACTORY MANAGER'S ATTENTION...
WHAT'S GOING ON HERE? CAN I HELP YOU, O' CHAMPION OF SAUSAGOPOLIS?
YOU CERTAINLY CAN. I NEED ONE OF YOUR BEST KIDNEYS.
WELL, IF YOU WANT ONE OF OUR VERY BEST, YOUR IN FOR A BIT OF TROUBLE. COME AND I'LL SHOW YOU WHERE WE GET THEM FROM.
...THE MANAGER LEADS OUR HEROES OUTSIDE...
HERE WE ARE. ALL OUR JUICIEST KIDNEYS ARE AT THE TOP OF THIS BEANSTALK!
SUPER.
LET ME GUESS. AN EVIL GIANT LIVES IN A CASTLE AT THE TOP, RIGHT?
I'M NOT SURE. ALL I KNOW IS THAT THERE'S KIDNEY'S FOR ALL!
THAT'S ALL WE NEEDED TO KNOW. LET'S GO, BILL. TIME IS OF THE ESSENCE!
YOU GO AHEAD. I'M SURE LITTLE JOHNNY WON'T MIND IF I SIT THIS ONE OUT.
BUT GLAME WILL NOT HEAR OF BILL'S FEEBLE EXCUSES AND SOON THE TWO ARE CLIMBING HIGH.
WOW! I CAN EVEN SEE OUR HOUSE FROM UP HERE!
YOU KNOW THAT FACTORY MANAGER WINKED AT ME? I THINK HE MIGHT BE GAY.
FINALLY THEY REACH THE TOP...
PHEW! HERE WE ARE, AT LAST.
HMM, YES. AND I SENSE A BAD FAIRY TALE PARODY IS ABOUT TO TAKE PLACE.
LOOK GLAME! IN THE DISTANCE—
YES, BILL. JUST AS YOU SUSPECTED. IT'S THE CASTLE OF A BRUTISH GIANT.
SO THE TWO HEROES SET OFF TO FACE THIS NEW FOE...
THIS GIANT BETTER HAVE A KIDNEY FOR POOR LITTLE JOHNNY OR I'LL CUT ONE OUT OF HIS OWN BLOODIED CORPSE.
YOU'RE A TRUE HUMANITARIAN, SIR GLAME.

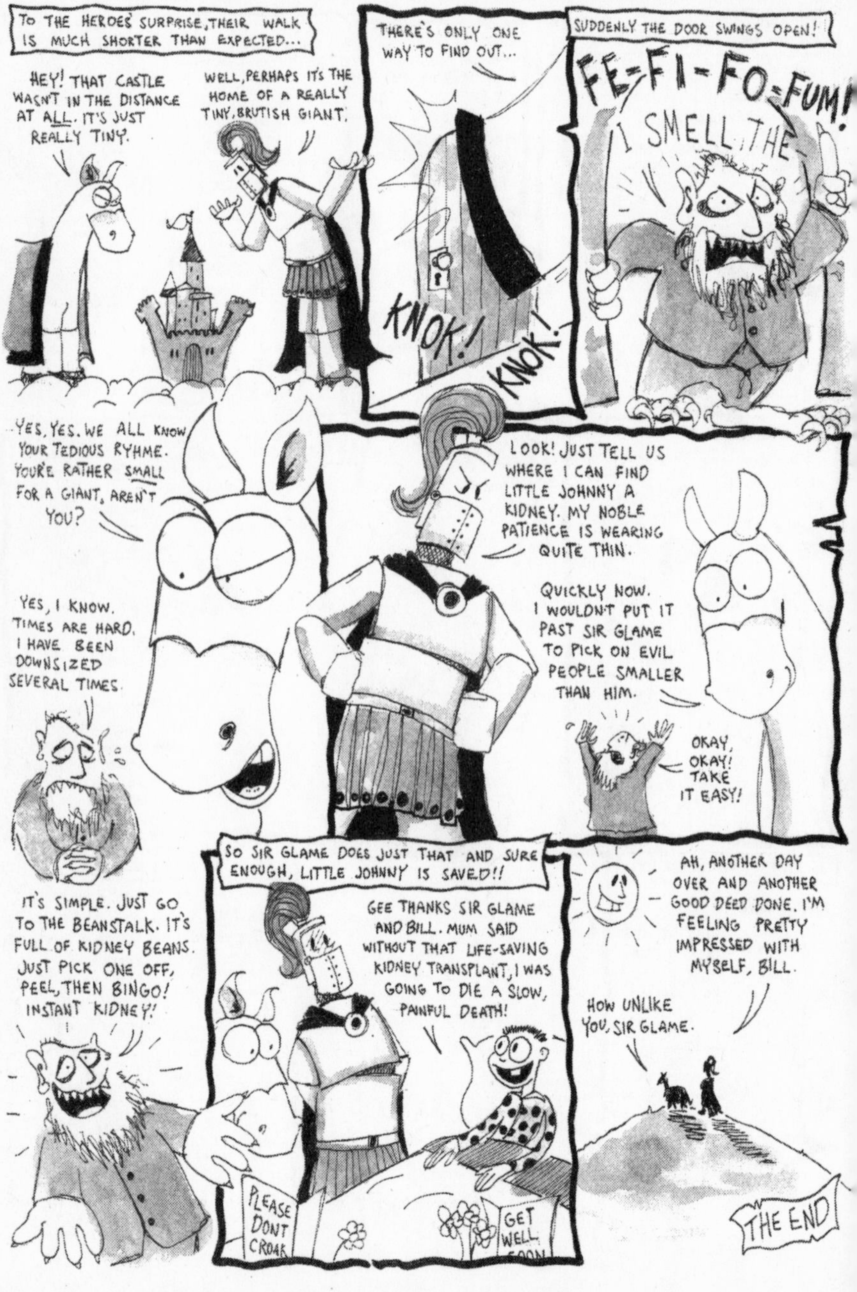
TO THE HEROES' SURPRISE, THEIR WALK IS MUCH SHORTER THAN EXPECTED...
HEY! THAT CASTLE WASN'T IN THE DISTANCE AT ALL. IT'S JUST REALLY TINY.
WELL, PERHAPS IT'S THE HOME OF A REALLY TINY, BRUTISH GIANT.
THERE'S ONLY ONE WAY TO FIND OUT...
KNOK! KNOK!
SUDDENLY THE DOOR SWINGS OPEN!
FE-FI-FO-FUM! I SMELL THE
YES, YES. WE ALL KNOW YOUR TEDIOUS RYHME. YOU'RE RATHER SMALL FOR A GIANT, AREN'T YOU?
YES, I KNOW. TIMES ARE HARD. I HAVE BEEN DOWNSIZED SEVERAL TIMES.
LOOK! JUST TELL US WHERE I CAN FIND LITTLE JOHNNY A KIDNEY. MY NOBLE PATIENCE IS WEARING QUITE THIN.
QUICKLY NOW. I WOULDN'T PUT IT PAST SIR GLAME TO PICK ON EVIL PEOPLE SMALLER THAN HIM.
OKAY, OKAY! TAKE IT EASY!
IT'S SIMPLE. JUST GO TO THE BEANSTALK. IT'S FULL OF KIDNEY BEANS. JUST PICK ONE OFF, PEEL, THEN BINGO! INSTANT KIDNEY!
SO SIR GLAME DOES JUST THAT AND SURE ENOUGH, LITTLE JOHNNY IS SAVED!!
GEE THANKS SIR GLAME AND BILL. MUM SAID WITHOUT THAT LIFE-SAVING KIDNEY TRANSPLANT, I WAS GOING TO DIE A SLOW, PAINFUL DEATH!
PLEASE DONT CROAK
GET WELL
AH, ANOTHER DAY OVER AND ANOTHER GOOD DEED DONE. I'M FEELING PRETTY IMPRESSED WITH MYSELF, BILL.
HOW UNLIKE YOU, SIR GLAME.
THE END

Chapter X

THEY'RE BACK AGAIN?

WELL, THERE GOES THE NEIGHBOURHOOD.

DID YOU SAY SOMETHING, BILL?

NO ENTRY

Sir Glame and Bill hurried across the courtyard, the dark castle looming over them.

Glame examined the truck.

'This is definitely the vehicle that ran us down. Notice it's still got the impression of my head mashed into the grill.'

'I'm noticing,' said Bill.

The front door to the castle had a big sign on it that read: *NO ENTRY*.

'Look, Bill! The sign is written in the same

THIS IS FOR RUNNING OVER MY HEAD!

SPLERK! RENCLE! CHUNKA! CREKCH!

ERR, GLAME? I'M NOT SURE IT'S TECHNICALLY POSSIBLE TO 'SLAY' INANIMATE OBJECTS.

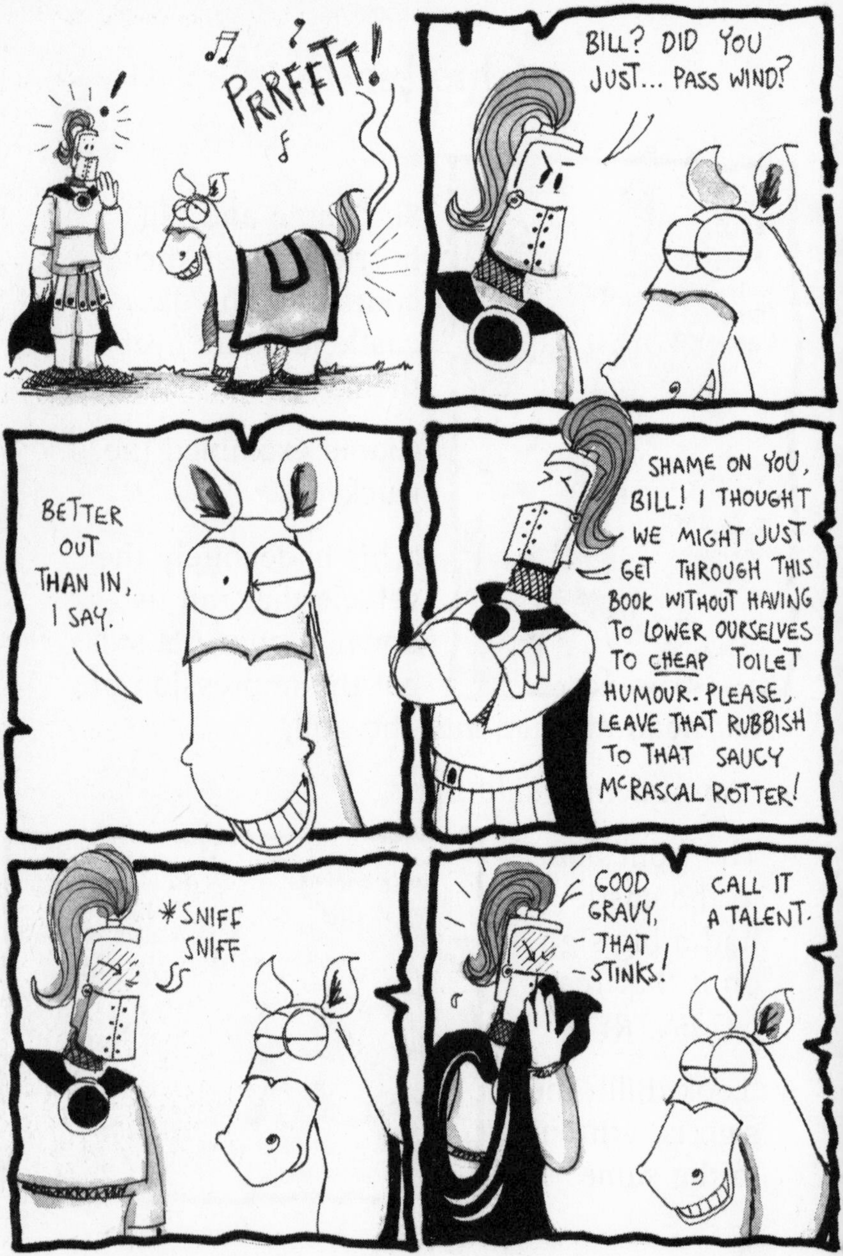
PRRFFTT!
BILL? DID YOU JUST... PASS WIND?
BETTER OUT THAN IN, I SAY.
SHAME ON YOU, BILL! I THOUGHT WE MIGHT JUST GET THROUGH THIS BOOK WITHOUT HAVING TO LOWER OURSELVES TO CHEAP TOILET HUMOUR. PLEASE, LEAVE THAT RUBBISH TO THAT SAUCY McRASCAL ROTTER!
*SNIFF SNIFF
GOOD GRAVY, THAT STINKS!
CALL IT A TALENT.

evil handwriting as all the other messages!'

'I'm looking,' said Bill.

Naturally a puny 'no entry' sign wasn't going to stop our heroes. Sir Glame quickly figured out a plan.

'We can get in through this kitty-door,' he said, pushing open the swinging door at the bottom of the larger one. 'See? We'll fit easily.'

'I'm seeing,' said Bill.

The two heroes strolled in through the kitty-door. Bill was nervous about a cat that needed a door so big a horse could fit through it. He tried to put the thought out of his mind.

Inside was exactly what you'd expect to find in a mad scientist's castle. A long corridor led to a big stone room filled with bubbling experiments, beakers and test tubes of coloured liquid. There were bookshelves filled with dusty manuals, a large table in the middle of the room and a crazy old man in a lab coat shouting nutty comments to his deformed assistant.

'Look at it, it's one giant cliché,' said Bill. 'A complete rip-off of *Frankenstein*.'

'Not now, Bill.' Sir Glame drew his sword and swaggered forward.

'Excuse me, Doctor! I am Sir Glame, hero of Sausagopolis! I have come to ask you a few questions about your recent activities.'

The Doctor ignored him. Goggles, his assistant toddled over.

'Doctor Nameless is very busy now, sir,' he said. 'If you're here to sell something he is not interested. Thank you, and please enjoy a complimentary mint on your way out.'

He handed the knight a green lolly shaped like a bat. Bill got one shaped like a ghost.

Sir Glame shoved Goggles out of the way. 'I'm talking to *you*, doctor...' Suddenly he noticed that the handwriting on the Doc's notepad looked very familiar. 'Or should I call you Saucy McRascal?!'

The doctor looked up from his experiments.

'Some call me a villain, some call me a hero, my mother calls me Treasure – but you, Sir Glame, can call me...Your Majesty!'

Doctor Nameless whipped off his mask to reveal his true identity.

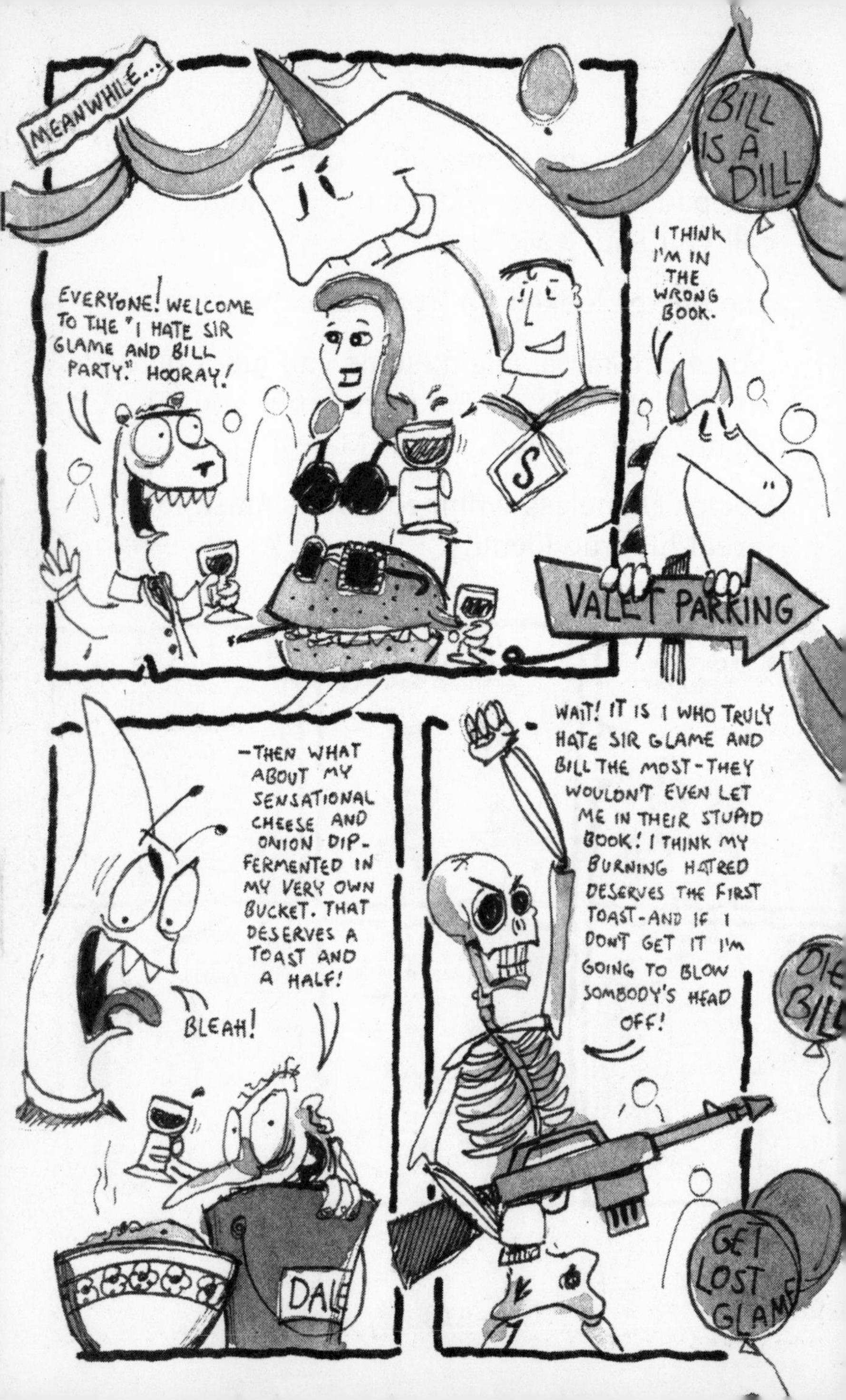
MEANWHILE...
BILL IS A DILL
EVERYONE! WELCOME TO THE "I HATE SIR GLAME AND BILL PARTY." HOORAY!
S
I THINK I'M IN THE WRONG BOOK.
VALET PARKING
-THEN WHAT ABOUT MY SENSATIONAL CHEESE AND ONION DIP-FERMENTED IN MY VERY OWN BUCKET. THAT DESERVES A TOAST AND A HALF!
BLEAH!
DALE
WAIT! IT IS I WHO TRULY HATE SIR GLAME AND BILL THE MOST-THEY WOULDN'T EVEN LET ME IN THEIR STUPID BOOK! I THINK MY BURNING HATRED DESERVES THE FIRST TOAST-AND IF I DON'T GET IT I'M GOING TO BLOW SOMBODY'S HEAD OFF!
GET LOST GLAME

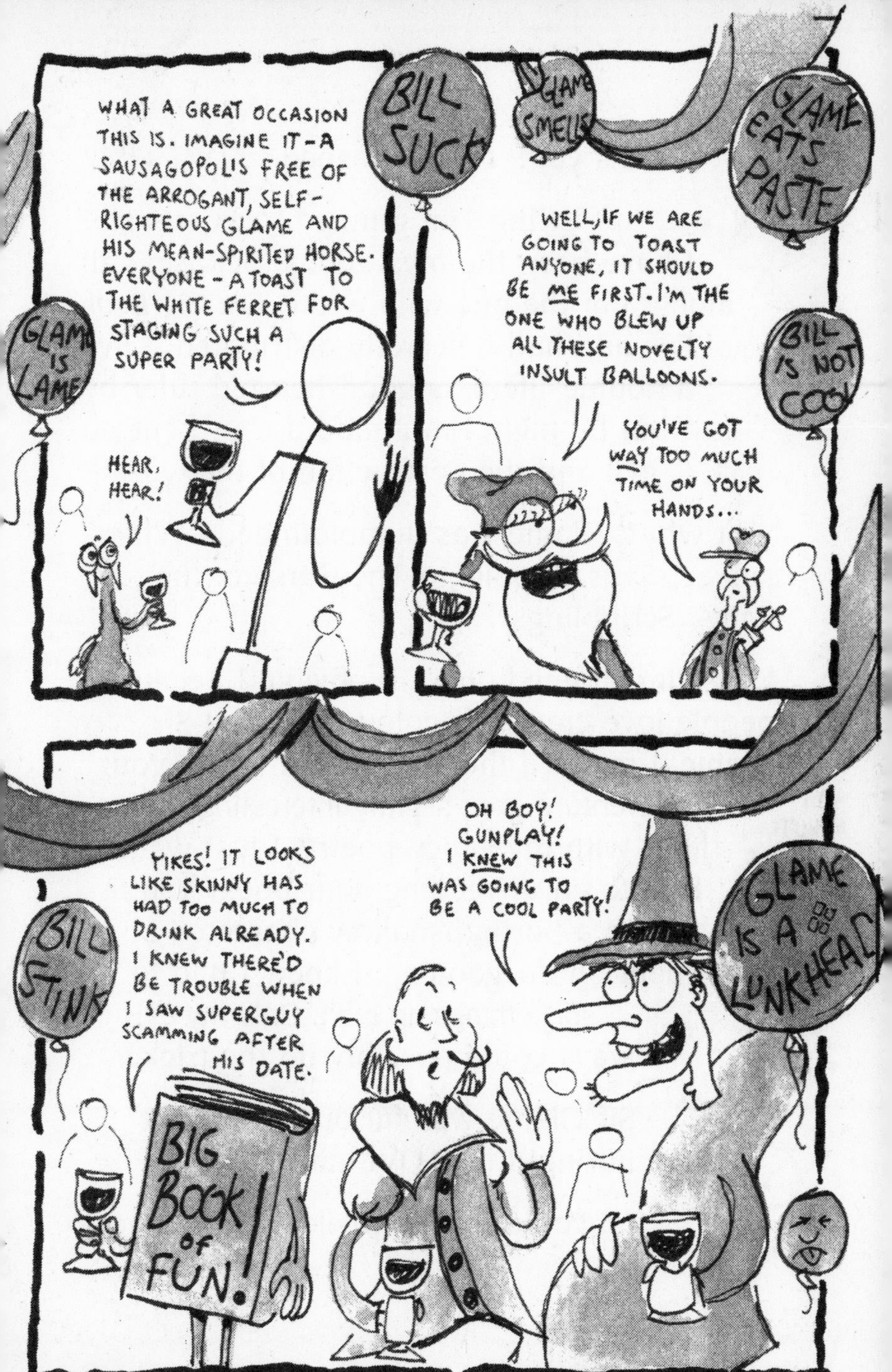
WHAT A GREAT OCCASION THIS IS. IMAGINE IT – A SAUSAGOPOLIS FREE OF THE ARROGANT, SELF-RIGHTEOUS GLAME AND HIS MEAN-SPIRITED HORSE. EVERYONE – A TOAST TO THE WHITE FERRET FOR STAGING SUCH A SUPER PARTY!
HEAR, HEAR!
GLAME IS LAME
BILL SUCK
GLAME SMELLS
GLAME EATS PASTE
WELL, IF WE ARE GOING TO TOAST ANYONE, IT SHOULD BE ME FIRST. I'M THE ONE WHO BLEW UP ALL THESE NOVELTY INSULT BALLOONS.
YOU'VE GOT WAY TOO MUCH TIME ON YOUR HANDS...
BILL IS NOT COOL
YIKES! IT LOOKS LIKE SKINNY HAS HAD TOO MUCH TO DRINK ALREADY. I KNEW THERE'D BE TROUBLE WHEN I SAW SUPERGUY SCAMMING AFTER HIS DATE.
OH BOY! GUNPLAY! I KNEW THIS WAS GOING TO BE A COOL PARTY!
BILL STINK
GLAME IS A LUNKHEAD
BIG BOOK of FUN!

'It's you!' Glame gasped. *'KING TIM!'*

King Tim grinned. 'Yes, it's me! I have been the mysterious McRascal all along! I'm the one who wrote *The Big Book of Fun* and had it secretly distributed. I live a double-life as a good-hearted ruler by day, but by night I'm a mad doctor bent on evil and the destruction of the world!'

'But why?' Glame was dumbfounded. 'Why subject Sausagopolis to The Curse of the Saucy Scribblings?'

King Tim laughed. 'Isn't it obvious? Because people love crass, off-colour humour! Sir Glame, I realised the only way to make your adventure even slightly interesting was to fill it with my saucy poetry. I just wanted kids to enjoy reading your book. You're such a boring, shallow character, so bent on do-gooding, I knew I had to spice things up a bit. Only my evil ways could possibly do the trick.'

Sir Glame was furious. 'I am not boring! Kids LOVE me!'

Bill could not keep silent any longer.

WAIT A MINUTE. IF IT WAS KING TIM ALL ALONG, DOES THIS MEAN I WON'T BE GETTING PAID?

BILL IS A JERK

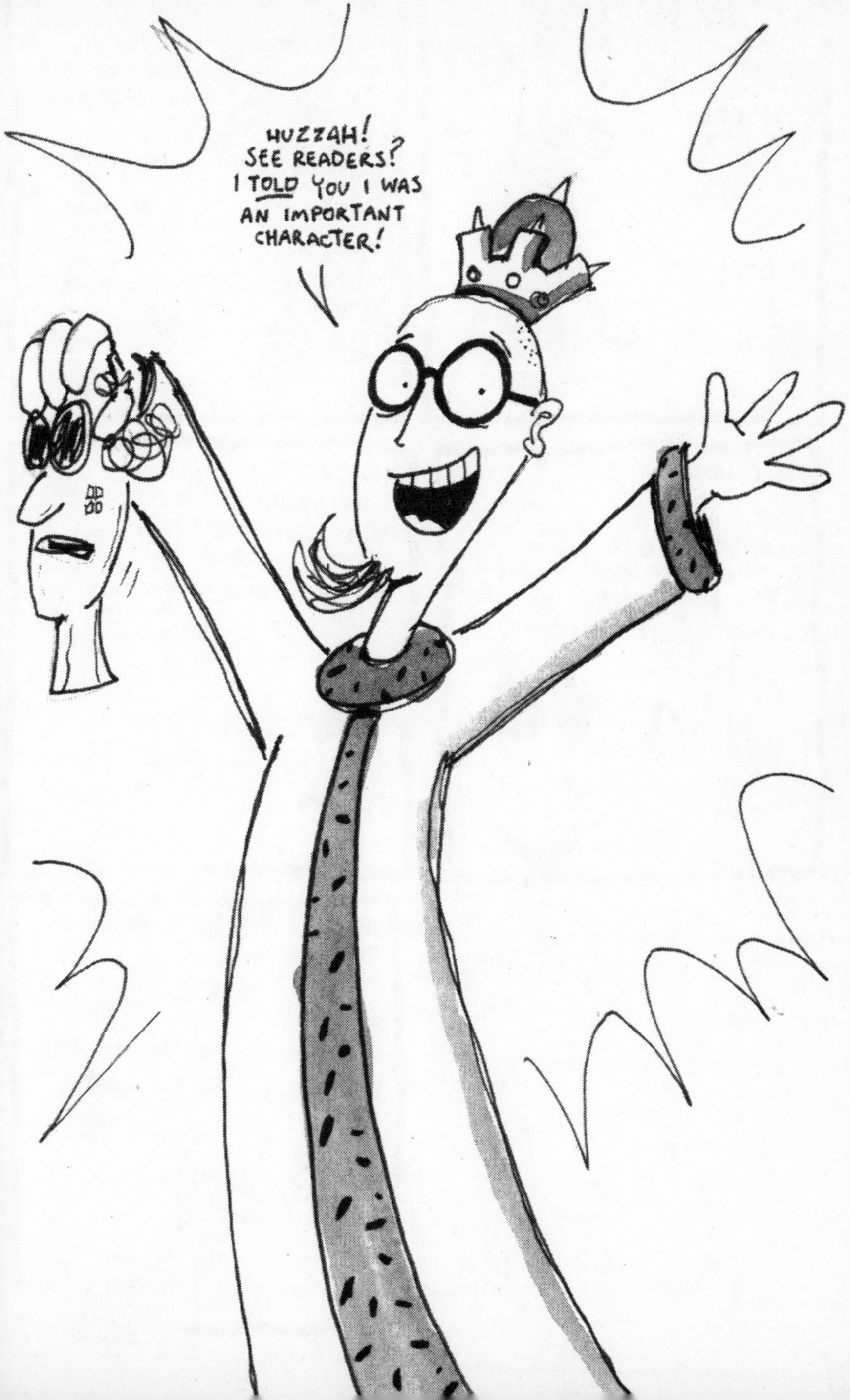
HUZZAH! SEE READERS? I TOLD YOU I WAS AN IMPORTANT CHARACTER!

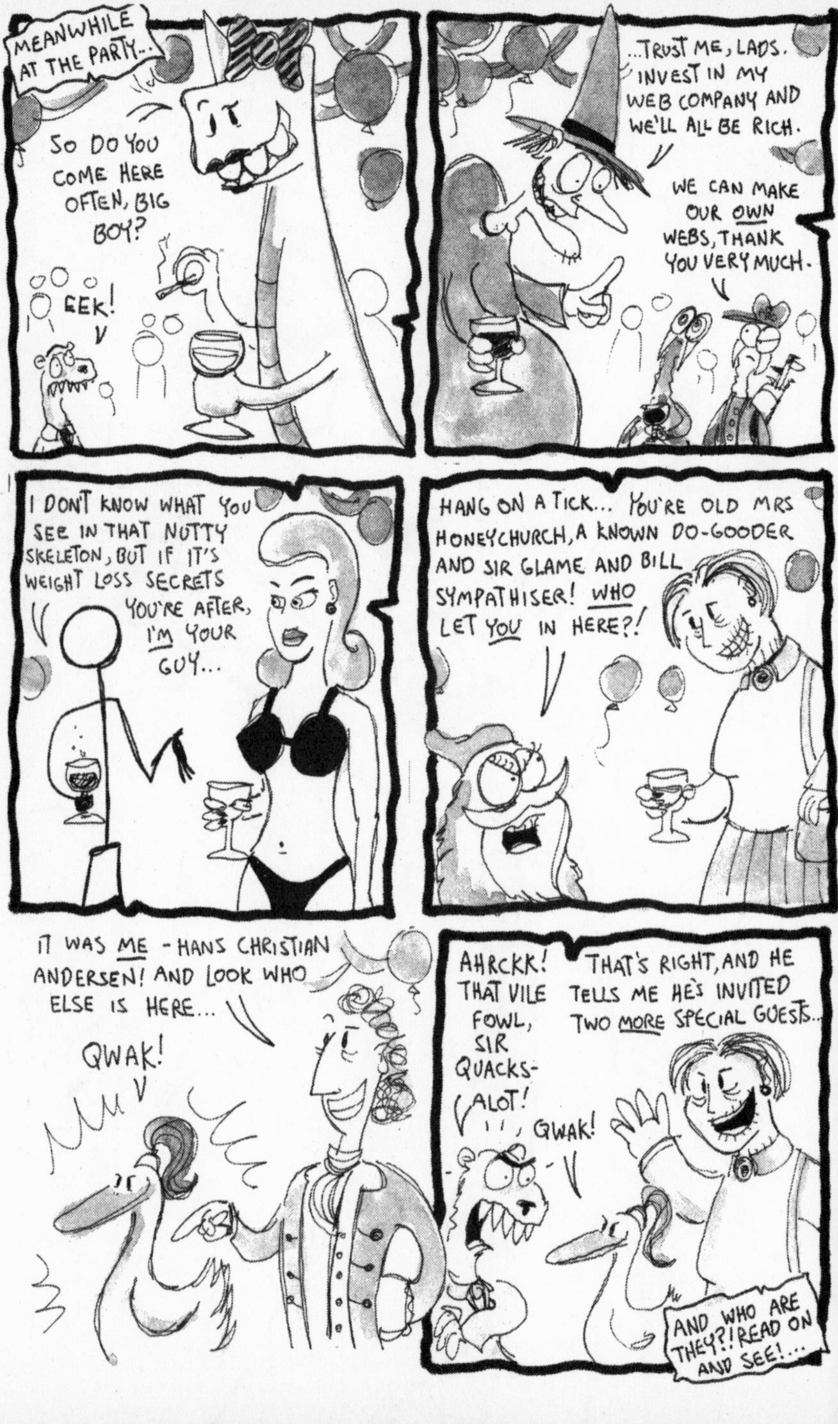
MEANWHILE AT THE PARTY...
SO DO YOU COME HERE OFTEN, BIG BOY?
EEK!
...TRUST ME, LADS. INVEST IN MY WEB COMPANY AND WE'LL ALL BE RICH.
WE CAN MAKE OUR OWN WEBS, THANK YOU VERY MUCH.
I DON'T KNOW WHAT YOU SEE IN THAT NUTTY SKELETON, BUT IF IT'S WEIGHT LOSS SECRETS YOU'RE AFTER, I'M YOUR GUY...
HANG ON A TICK... YOU'RE OLD MRS HONEYCHURCH, A KNOWN DO-GOODER AND SIR GLAME AND BILL SYMPATHISER! WHO LET YOU IN HERE?!
IT WAS ME - HANS CHRISTIAN ANDERSEN! AND LOOK WHO ELSE IS HERE...
QWAK!
AHRCKK! THAT VILE FOWL, SIR QUACKS-ALOT!
THAT'S RIGHT, AND HE TELLS ME HE'S INVITED TWO MORE SPECIAL GUESTS...
QWAK!
AND WHO ARE THEY?! READ ON AND SEE!...

'Okay, I've had about all I can take. I knew our whole adventure was contrived by some weak-minded fool, but I never thought it would end *this* badly! King Tim, you've obviously eaten one too many ornamental bath soaps to come up with such a sorry excuse for a quest. The fact you have no real motive and this book's entire story is full of holes – it's too hard to ignore!'

'Now wait, Bill,' said Glame. 'Don't you think King Tim turning out to be the villain all along was a surprising plot twist? I never guessed it myself. I think you're being too hard on us.'

'Yes, come now Bill,' said King Tim. 'I know you love my poetry. Here – listen to my latest one:

> *There was a tiny guinea-pig*
> *Who being small, was not that big*
> *He lived with his pal the elephant*
> *Who being huge, was not that scant.*
> *They would sit together on the couch*
> *And listen to each other grouch*
> *About the price of straw and hay*

And the cost of living in the everyday.
Yet once when Elephant sat with his friend
Forgetting his place he took the wrong end.
For Guinea-pig it now is much less fun
To chat from inside an elephant's bum.'

'That's awful!' Sir Glame growled. 'How dare you bring your toilet wit into my fantasy setting. You're poisoning innocent minds with that smutty smut. As my King I'm

supposed to obey you, but as the villain, I'm expected to hack you to pieces!'

'Look, let's just all face facts,' Bill groaned. 'It's time somebody said it: THIS BOOK SUCKS!'

'That's it, Bill! I try and try to make our adventures interesting and exciting, but you constantly tear us down! All your complaining and smarmy remarks, I've had it with you! You're not a team player and you don't care about anyone but yourself! I'm going to fill out a *Strike Three* form and hand it in to King Tim right now! That's Three Strikes, and that means you're OUT!'

'Out of *what*?' Bill grabbed the forms out of Glame's hands and tore them up. 'Your stupid forms mean nothing! I say *you're* OUT!'

Sir Glame was shocked. 'Look what you've done! Destroying official documents is a Strike Three offence!'

'Oh yes? Then what about this?' and Bill read a vintage piece of Saucy McRascal:

'Johnny Jones, the right little twerp
Was a naughty boy who did a big loud burp
His belch had such clout
His guts he spewed out
So he sucked them back in with a slurp.

Sir Glame covered his ears. 'No! Stop! Our book must remain pure!'

'There!' Bill declared, 'There's some gutter humour for you. You still think this story is any good now?'

UH OH!
HERE IT
COMES—
HE'S GOING
TO BLOW!

Sir Glame's armour began heating up. He was really mad now. The knight threw himself at Bill.

'Arrggghhh!!! I can't take it! The whole world is against me!'

Bill ducked out of the way and Glame crashed into one of the Doctor's wacky machines. The device suddenly sparked to life and shot a science-fictiony looking beam at the knight.

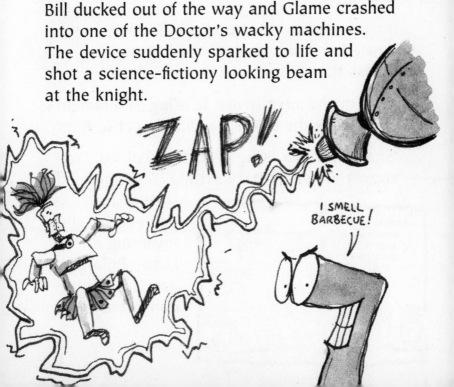

'No!' King Tim cried. 'Not my Enlarge-o Ray!'

In an instant, Sir Glame was blown up to eighty-three times his normal size. The colossal knight's head smashed through the ceiling.

'I can't take it any more!' Sir Glame howled and stomped off the mountain across the countryside.

'Oh boy, he's really lost it,' King Tim lamented. 'I think the stress has finally got to him.'

'Shame on you, King Tim,' Bill scolded. 'You know this is a fantasy setting. Bringing mad science into it is bad enough, but inventing a hokey Enlarge-o Ray is just plain dangerous.'

King Tim drooped. 'What do you think Glame's going to do?'

'If I know Sir Glame, he'll work his frustrations out in a violent, destructive manner.' Bill ran over to the ray machine. 'And there's only one way to stop a 500 foot tall knight on a rampage.' He flicked the 'on' switch. 'And that's with a 500 foot tall horse to bring him down!'

The ray zapped over him, and Bill blew up to a fantastically huge size. He stomped out onto the mountain.

'And by the way, King Tim,' he thundered down. 'This is for wasting everyone's time,' and he stepped on the castle, smashing it completely. 'Especially mine.'

King Tim crawled out of the rubble.

'Sorry, Bill.'

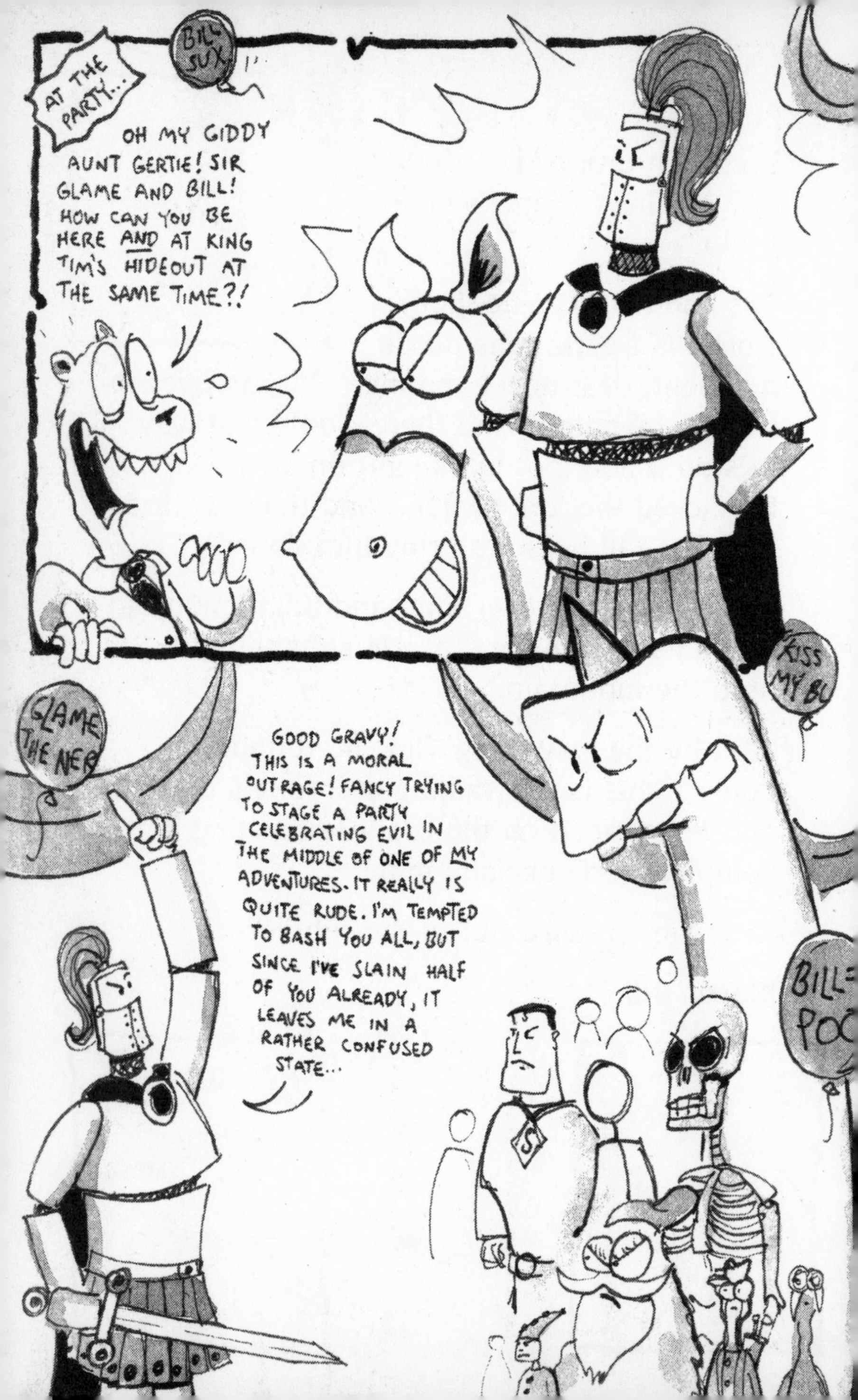
AT THE PARTY...
BILL SUX
OH MY GIDDY AUNT GERTIE! SIR GLAME AND BILL! HOW CAN YOU BE HERE AND AT KING TIM'S HIDEOUT AT THE SAME TIME?!
KISS MY BU
GLAME THE NER
GOOD GRAVY! THIS IS A MORAL OUTRAGE! FANCY TRYING TO STAGE A PARTY CELEBRATING EVIL IN THE MIDDLE OF ONE OF MY ADVENTURES. IT REALLY IS QUITE RUDE. I'M TEMPTED TO BASH YOU ALL, BUT SINCE I'VE SLAIN HALF OF YOU ALREADY, IT LEAVES ME IN A RATHER CONFUSED STATE...
BILL= POO

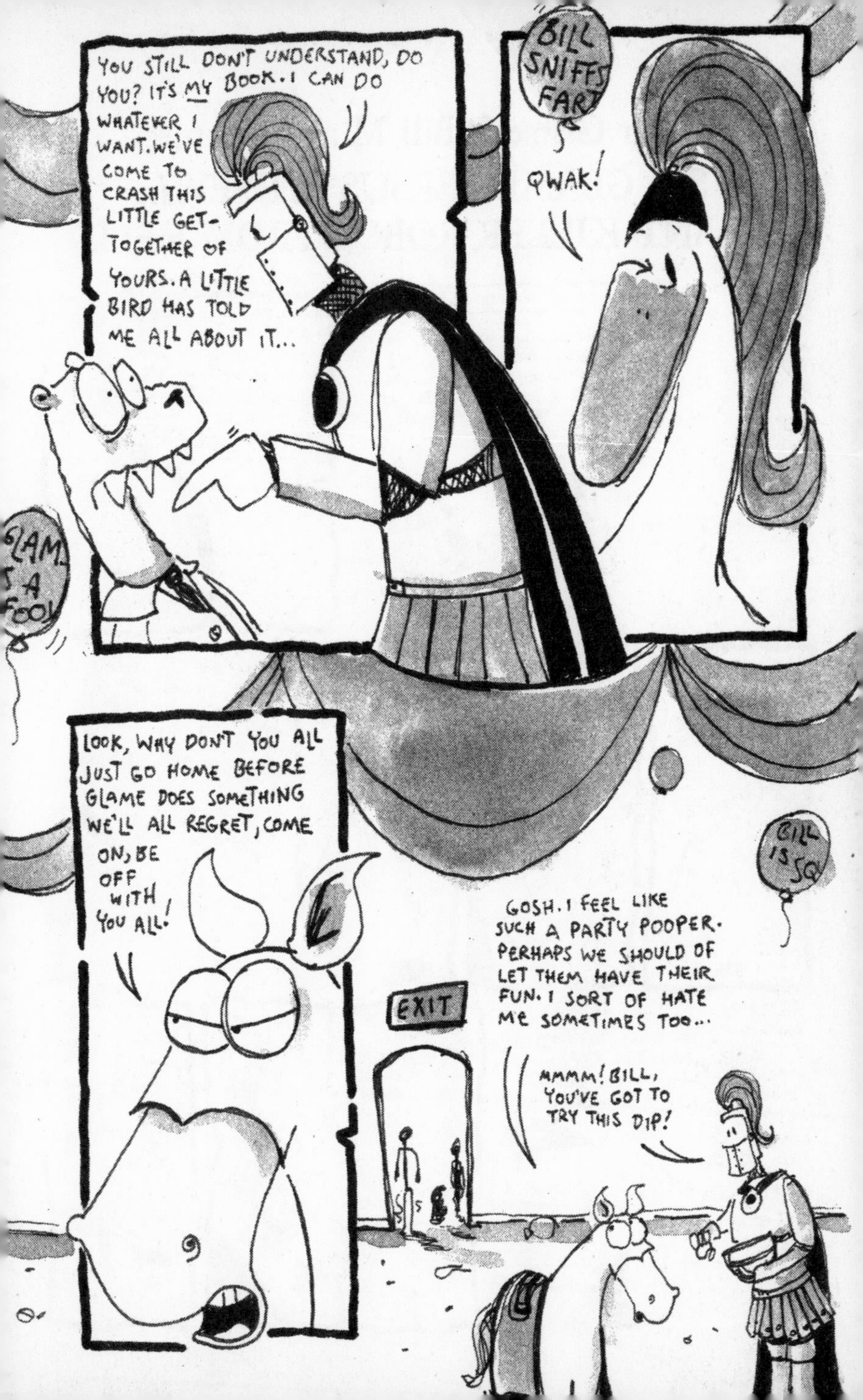

YOU STILL DON'T UNDERSTAND, DO YOU? IT'S MY BOOK. I CAN DO WHATEVER I WANT. WE'VE COME TO CRASH THIS LITTLE GET-TOGETHER OF YOURS. A LITTLE BIRD HAS TOLD ME ALL ABOUT IT...
BILL SNIFFS FART
QWAK!
LOOK, WHY DON'T YOU ALL JUST GO HOME BEFORE GLAME DOES SOMETHING WE'LL ALL REGRET, COME ON, BE OFF WITH YOU ALL!
EXIT
GOSH. I FEEL LIKE SUCH A PARTY POOPER. PERHAPS WE SHOULD OF LET THEM HAVE THEIR FUN. I SORT OF HATE ME SOMETIMES TOO...
MMMM! BILL, YOU'VE GOT TO TRY THIS DIP!

A Sir Glame & Bill Mini-Adventure
SIR GLAME VERSUS THE EVIL, GIANT KILLER ROBOT FROM HELL

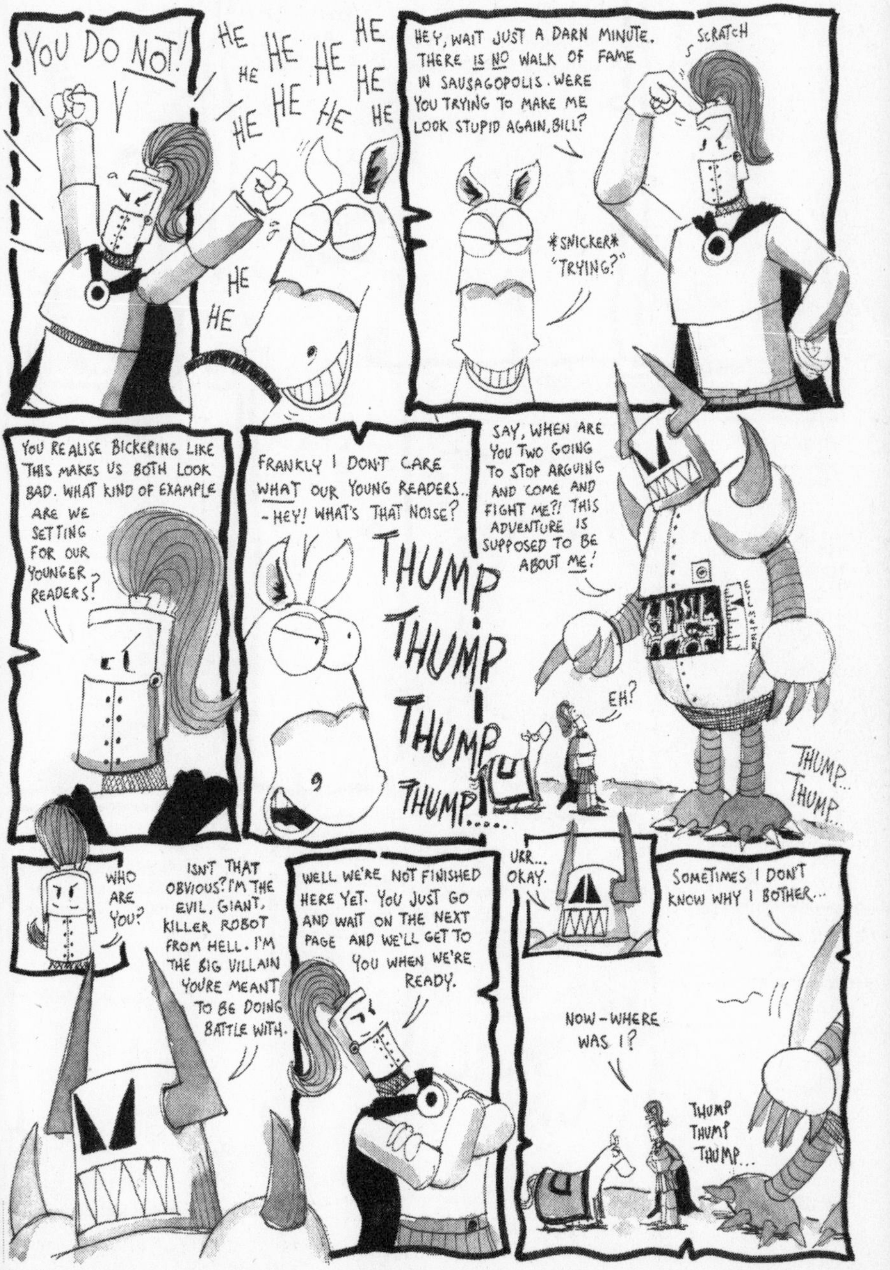

YOU DO NOT!
HE HE HE HE HE HE HE HE HE HE
HE HE
HEY, WAIT JUST A DARN MINUTE. THERE IS NO WALK OF FAME IN SAUSAGOPOLIS. WERE YOU TRYING TO MAKE ME LOOK STUPID AGAIN, BILL?
SCRATCH
SNICKER "TRYING?"
YOU REALISE BICKERING LIKE THIS MAKES US BOTH LOOK BAD. WHAT KIND OF EXAMPLE ARE WE SETTING FOR OUR YOUNGER READERS?
FRANKLY I DON'T CARE WHAT OUR YOUNG READERS... - HEY! WHAT'S THAT NOISE?
THUMP THUMP THUMP THUMP....
SAY, WHEN ARE YOU TWO GOING TO STOP ARGUING AND COME AND FIGHT ME?! THIS ADVENTURE IS SUPPOSED TO BE ABOUT ME!
EH?
THUMP... THUMP...
WHO ARE YOU?
ISN'T THAT OBVIOUS? I'M THE EVIL, GIANT, KILLER ROBOT FROM HELL. I'M THE BIG VILLAIN YOU'RE MEANT TO BE DOING BATTLE WITH.
WELL WE'RE NOT FINISHED HERE YET. YOU JUST GO AND WAIT ON THE NEXT PAGE AND WE'LL GET TO YOU WHEN WE'RE READY.
URR... OKAY.
SOMETIMES I DON'T KNOW WHY I BOTHER...
NOW - WHERE WAS I?
THUMP THUMP THUMP...

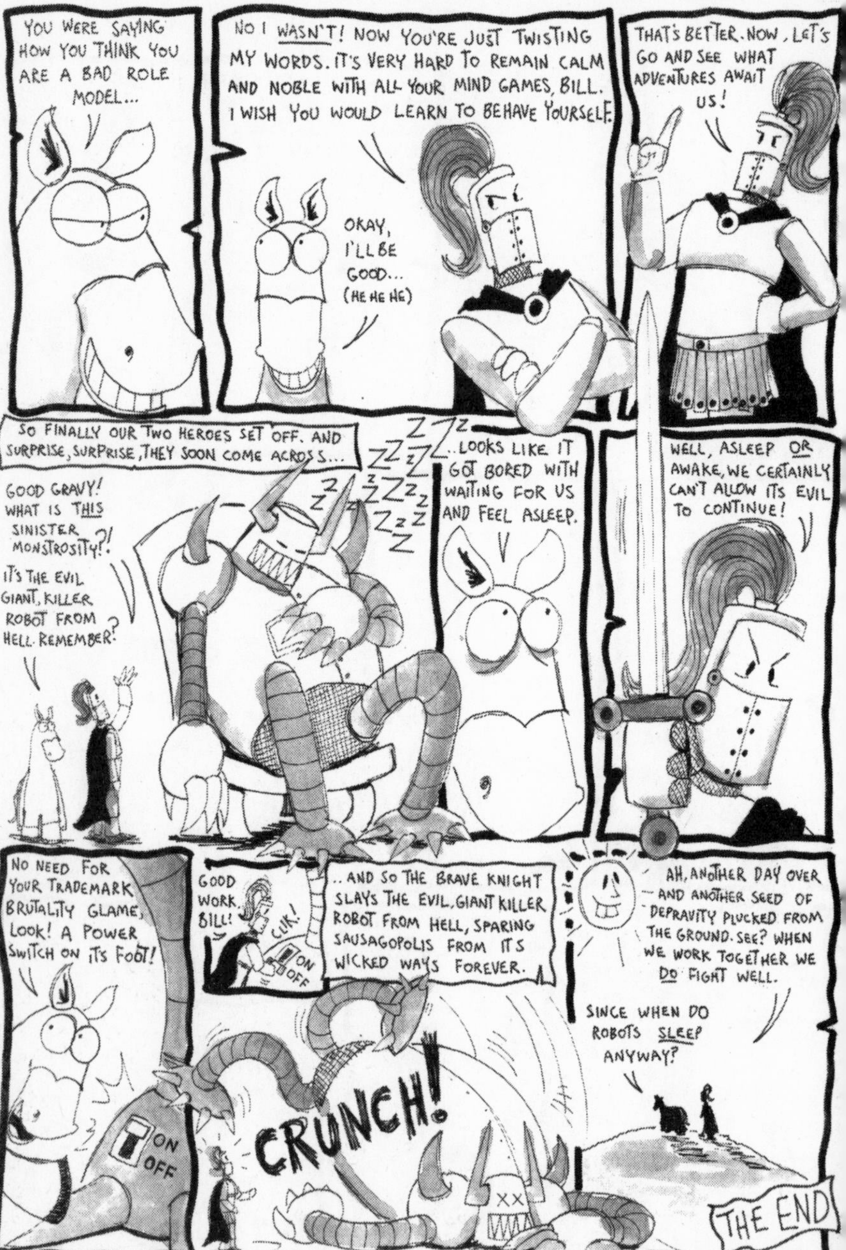
YOU WERE SAYING HOW YOU THINK YOU ARE A BAD ROLE MODEL...
NO I WASN'T! NOW YOU'RE JUST TWISTING MY WORDS. IT'S VERY HARD TO REMAIN CALM AND NOBLE WITH ALL YOUR MIND GAMES, BILL. I WISH YOU WOULD LEARN TO BEHAVE YOURSELF.
OKAY, I'LL BE GOOD... (HE HE HE)
THAT'S BETTER. NOW, LET'S GO AND SEE WHAT ADVENTURES AWAIT US!
SO FINALLY OUR TWO HEROES SET OFF. AND SURPRISE, SURPRISE, THEY SOON COME ACROSS...
GOOD GRAVY! WHAT IS THIS SINISTER MONSTROSITY?!
IT'S THE EVIL GIANT, KILLER ROBOT FROM HELL. REMEMBER?
ZZZ
..LOOKS LIKE IT GOT BORED WITH WAITING FOR US AND FEEL ASLEEP.
WELL, ASLEEP OR AWAKE, WE CERTAINLY CAN'T ALLOW ITS EVIL TO CONTINUE!
NO NEED FOR YOUR TRADEMARK BRUTALITY GLAME, LOOK! A POWER SWITCH ON IT'S FOOT!
ON
OFF
GOOD WORK, BILL!
CLIK!
ON
OFF
..AND SO THE BRAVE KNIGHT SLAYS THE EVIL, GIANT KILLER ROBOT FROM HELL, SPARING SAUSAGOPOLIS FROM ITS WICKED WAYS FOREVER.
CRUNCH!
AH, ANOTHER DAY OVER AND ANOTHER SEED OF DEPRAVITY PLUCKED FROM THE GROUND. SEE? WHEN WE WORK TOGETHER WE DO FIGHT WELL.
SINCE WHEN DO ROBOTS SLEEP ANYWAY?
THE END

One Chapter Too Many

Bill pounded across the countryside, each stride miles long. Stepping across the Great Forest and hopping over the Great Desert, he soon spotted Sir Glame's immense shape standing in the middle of Sausagopolis's capital. The knight was smashing the city to pieces.

'Sir Glame!' Bill called. 'What are you doing?'

'I'm wrecking Sausagopolis, Bill! Don't try and stop me!' Sir Glame kicked the City Library across town. 'There! That's for not letting me borrow those large print books without a disability card!'

'By why wreck Sausagopolis?' said Bill. 'This city loves you!'

'No it doesn't. This whole country is one giant joke and I always seem to be the butt of it. Nobody takes anything seriously, so why should I?'

Bill crunched down main street. Beneath him citizens ran screaming for cover. 'I can't let you, Glame! This is my town too!'

'You should talk!' the knight declared. 'You're the most sarcastic of all! I would have thought you'd love to wreck this ridiculous excuse for a fairytale world. We've got computers and cars and evil scientists – it's absurd. And everybody pretends like it's fine. Well, it's not, and it's time I did some spring cleaning!'

'Don't you *touch* this place. This is my fantasy setting too.'

'Oh yes? And who's going to stop me? YOU?'

'You know it, sister!' Bill picked up City Hall and smashed it over Glame's head. 'It's about time we had a showdown!'

Sir Glame punched him in the guts. Bill tripped over the palace and fell on the city park.

'Owww! The park fountain is sticking me in the butt!'

Sir Glame picked up a handful of townsfolk and mashed them in Bill's face. 'Kiss the people if you love them so much!'

Bill spat them out. 'Yuck!' He kicked Sir Glame in the privates.

'Oww, right in the tacklebox!'
Glame fell back and groaned.
'So, you want to get low, do you?'

Glame ripped the steeple off the city church and stabbed Bill in the spine. 'There! *That's* for having to listen to you this entire book!'

'Ouch!' cried Bill. 'My vertebrae! So, you think only *you* can fight dirty?!'

Bill pulled a long sewer tunnel out of the ground like a tree root. He shoved it inside Glame's visor. 'Drink that, you windbag! See what it's like to have rubbish go *back in* your mouth for a change!'

Sir Glame collapsed, coughing and gasping for air. 'Beelcch! You've poisoned me you dirty horse!'

'So? What about what you've done to me?!' Bill looked at the church steeple sticking out of his side and fainted.

Sir Glame took long gulps out of the city river but it was no use. He vomited up an ocean and then promptly passed out.

IS THIS THE END FOR OUR HEROES?

I SURE HOPE SO!

The two 500 foot heroes lay side by side in the middle of the smashed Sausagopolis. The dust began to settle. Soon townsfolk came out from hiding to examine the damage. They saw their fallen champions unconscious and defeated. It didn't take long to decide what had to be done.

*   *   *

So, young readers? What do you think happened to our heroes, Sir Glame and Bill, when everything was over? What would you do to a person you thought was nice but ended up smashing your town?

King Tim had just that dilemma. Luckily nobody ever found out about his secret double life as the sinister Doctor Nameless who was actually Saucy McRascal in disguise. He had to put his dark side on hold anyway. Since Bill had stepped on his remote headquarters there was nowhere he could go to relax and be evil in private.

I SUPPOSE I'LL HAVE TO HALT MY NAUGHTY WAYS FOR A WHILE. THANK HEAVENS I KEPT MY DAY JOB.

As for The Curse of the Saucy Scribblings, Bill was right all along. It wasn't really a curse, it was just a passing fad. Folk soon got sick of reading bawdy, lowbrow poetry and moved onto the next Sausagopolis craze – hula hoops. It was never explained why King Tim enjoyed being evil so much, but that isn't really important to the story, is it?

'Yes, it is!' growled Bill. 'It's very important. It's proof that this whole book is a no-talent, no-imagination farce!'

Please, pay no attention to Bill. He is just upset that he and Sir Glame were thrown in a mental hospital.

After being shrunk back down to normal size, the two were committed to The Brothers Dimm Home for the Heroically Insane. Sir Glame was forced to use an iron lung machine to breathe because of the acute sewer poisoning. Bill ended up in a wheelchair thanks to spinal damage from that church steeple.

The two ex-heroes sat playing Scrabble in the hospital lounge.

'I hope you're happy, Bill. You finally drove me over the edge with all your sarcasm and complaining. How could I have possibly maintained my noble spirit listening to you? Now I'm stuck to this accursed life support machine if I want to keep breathing.'

'Why should I feel sorry for you? I'm crippled!'

'Not crippled, Bill – physically challenged.'

QWAK!

'Whatever,' Bill rolled his eyes. 'At least I proved one thing: that this whole book was *truly* plotless, pointless and pathetic.'

Sir Glame smiled. 'You're so bitter. You need to chin up. I myself refuse to give in. I have a feeling this isn't the end for us. I *will* be Sausagopolis's number one hero again. You mark my words.'

SAUSAGOPOLIS'S NEW Nº 1 HERO

'I'd like to see that,' Bill chuckled. 'Me wheeling around and you dragging your respirator into battle.'

Sir Glame shrugged. 'I'm sure we'll get better eventually.'

Bill looked around nervously. He had a sneaking suspicion Sir Glame was right.

The End

'The end,' sighed Bill. 'Phew! At last it's finally finished.'

'Checkmate!' Sir Glame clapped his hands.

Bill looked down at the game board. 'We're playing Scrabble, not chess!'

'So when do I pass go and collect $200?'

The horse groaned. The book had ended, but his suffering would go on long after the reading was over.

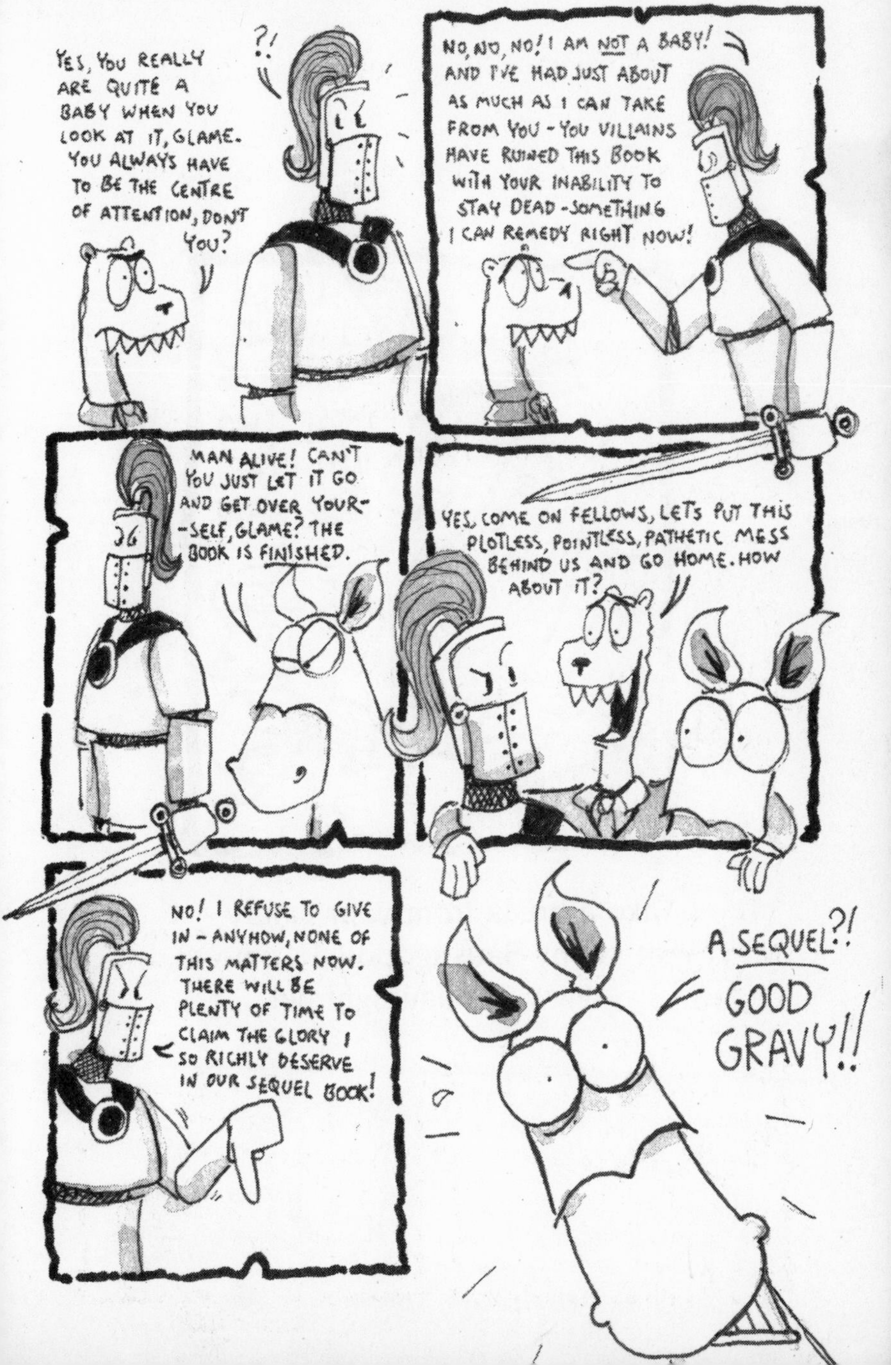
YES, YOU REALLY ARE QUITE A BABY WHEN YOU LOOK AT IT, GLAME. YOU ALWAYS HAVE TO BE THE CENTRE OF ATTENTION, DONT YOU?
?!
NO, NO, NO! I AM NOT A BABY! AND I'VE HAD JUST ABOUT AS MUCH AS I CAN TAKE FROM YOU - YOU VILLAINS HAVE RUINED THIS BOOK WITH YOUR INABILITY TO STAY DEAD - SOMETHING I CAN REMEDY RIGHT NOW!
MAN ALIVE! CAN'T YOU JUST LET IT GO AND GET OVER YOUR--SELF, GLAME? THE BOOK IS FINISHED.
YES, COME ON FELLOWS, LETS PUT THIS PLOTLESS, POINTLESS, PATHETIC MESS BEHIND US AND GO HOME. HOW ABOUT IT?
NO! I REFUSE TO GIVE IN - ANYHOW, NONE OF THIS MATTERS NOW. THERE WILL BE PLENTY OF TIME TO CLAIM THE GLORY I SO RICHLY DESERVE IN OUR SEQUEL BOOK!
A SEQUEL?! GOOD GRAVY!!

Take a break from your sanity –
visit sunny Sausagopolis! Come to
www.Joshuawright.net